CROWNING GLORY

"I crown you Rellard," Georgie intoned, "Keeper of the Power. The Power of the Water, the Power of the Fire, the Power of the Leaf and the Rock, of the Wing and Claw and Feather. Use them well, O Rellard."

He lowered the rough iron circlet onto Lucy's head, where it fitted exactly. Shelley knelt and presented the faded pillow that made a nest for the Orb. "I bestow upon you, O Rellard, the Power."

Lucy picked up the glass ball in both hands, raising it so that she was looking directly into the swirling spirals of color. "The Power is here," she whispered.

The Power of the Rellard

Carolyn F. Logan

BORZOI SPRINTERS • ALFRED A. KNOPF
New York

Dr. M. Jerry Weiss, Distinguished Service Professor of Communications at Jersey City State College, is the educational consultant for Borzoi Sprinters. A past chair of the International Reading Association President's Advisory Committee on Intellectual Freedom, he travels frequently to give workshops on the use of trade books in schools.

A BORZOI SPRINTER PUBLISHED BY ALFRED A. KNOPF, INC.
Copyright © 1986 by Carolyn F. Logan
Cover art copyright © 1989 by Doug Gray

Library of Congress Catalog Card Number: 87-22592
ISBN: 0-394-82586-1
RL: 5.2
First Borzoi Sprinter edition: September 1989

Manufactured in the United States of America
1   2   3   4   5   6   7   8   9   10

CONTENTS

ONE

The Gift

It all began as an amusement to fill the time while they were waiting to be well. A cold wind pushed their mother in at the front door. "Don't slam the door!" she would shout at them, but she always let it fall shut with a crash herself. Today she was pink with excitement.

"Look what I've found for you, you poor sick things. This will cheer you up!"

They were always sick together; it was more fun that way. Georgie usually had the most spots or the deepest cough or the highest fever. Lucy trailed along after, not as ill as Georgie but sick enough to guarantee bed rest and meals on trays. Shelley usually organized their convalescence because she was the oldest and naturally bossy.

But this time Lucy was very ill with a high fever. Doctor MacCreath said that she had a particularly vicious virus and sent Lucy away to the hospital for special care and tests.

"That should show us just what we're dealing with," Doctor MacCreath assured their mother when he came to check over Georgie and Shelley.

But Doctor MacCreath was wrong. The tests showed nothing conclusive.

"The virus seems to be affecting her nervous system in some way. I've never known this particular set of complications to occur. It's very strange, very strange," and he shook his head as he took Shelley's pulse.

"Lucy is going to get better, isn't she?" asked Georgie from the other bed. It was really Lucy's bed but Georgie had wanted to move in with Shelley when Lucy went to the hospital.

"It's lonely in my room," he told his mother, and she helped him move a few of his books and toys into the girls' room.

Doctor MacCreath turned to face the boy. "Of course," he said. "She'll be home soon," and he walked out of the bedroom and down the stairs, talking to their mother.

"He's lying!" Shelley leaned from the pillow to hiss at Georgie. "Lucy's sick, awfully sick."

"He can't lie," Georgie insisted. "He's a doctor."

" 'Course he can. He just doesn't want to worry us. Lucy's sick, all right."

"Will she die?"

"Maybe."

"What'll we do?"

"I don't know. I'll have to think."

Very late that afternoon, a call came from the hospital. Their mother was pale and trembling when she came to kiss them good-bye.

"Mrs. Dodds is downstairs. She'll bring you your trays soon. Be good now," and she rushed away, bumping blindly through the door, down the stairs and out to the waiting car, which was puffing little cold clouds of exhaust in the driveway. Dad beeped the horn twice for them as he drove off.

"She's going to die." Georgie's voice squeezed past the thickness in his throat. "Isn't she?"

"Maybe not."

"Can I come over with you?"

"Sure."

Georgie snuggled close under the blankets. He clasped Shelley's hand in his and breathed in deeply the lovely eucalyptus smell that enveloped his sister.

They huddled there quietly, the sound of the television thundering up the stairs and into their room. It was too loud because Mrs. Dodds was very deaf.

Profoundly deaf, Georgie always said. Pro-*found*ly!

"Let's sing to her."

"That won't make her turn the television down!" snorted Shelley.

"Not to Mrs. Dodds, not to her." Georgie's voice sank lower, almost to a whisper. "Let's sing for Lucy."

Shelley began to sing, her voice a clear true thread of sound weaving a web against the television laughter from below:

> *" 'Tis a gift to be simple,*
> *'tis a gift to be free."*

Georgie joined in with his bumblebee monotone:

> *" 'Tis a gift to come down*
> *where you ought to be.*
> *And when we find ourselves*
> *in the place just right,*
> *'Twill be in the valley*
> *of love and delight!"*

They sang it all the way through and then did "Michael, Row the Boat Ashore" twice. That one was slow and had hallelujah in it, which seemed to suit the occasion.

Then they sang other songs, all the songs they could remember. Songs from school, songs from television, songs from the movies, from Sunday School—parts of songs, made-up songs, half-remembered songs. They la-la-laed when they did not know the words and fitted in new notes where bits of the tune were missing. On and on they sang, not stopping. It seemed urgent not to stop, to sing on, to keep the music flowing out, a stream of music flowing through the cold twilight, out over the cold hills, out to Lucy. Huddled straight together, pushed back hard against the pillows, they sang on and on until Mrs. Dodds climbed the stairs with their suppers. Then they stopped, hoarse with their effort.

Much later, Mum came in to kiss them good night and pull up their covers. Her cheek was soft and cold.

"Lucy's going to be all right," she whispered. "Doctor MacCreath says she's turned the corner."

Georgie loved that phrase. "She's turned the corner!" he would murmur, savoring the *r*'s on his tongue.

But when Lucy came home and began to improve, it became apparent that the disease was not going to let her go entirely unscathed. Something had happened to the nerves in her right arm and hand and they were left twisted and withered.

Mum's find was an old game that she had dragged out from under a pile of shoes at Mrs. Penning's garage sale. Actually, it wasn't a game, it was a toy theater with some of the pieces missing. The three children immediately made it their own, weaving a strong web of fantasy around the dilapidated stage and the tawdry figures that no longer fitted snugly in their appointed slots. As time went by and Lucy began to get stronger, the game grew more and more elaborate. The stage became too small to contain their drama and the lean-to at the back of the garden shed was appropriated. The flimsy cardboard actors were discarded and the children themselves became the players.

"We'll keep this one, for the Rellard." Lucy strung a length of ribbon through a hole in the crown of one cardboard figure. "See?" She laughed. "A necklace!" The figure dangled from her neck, bobbing against her chest as she danced.

"Rellardo, lardo, do! do! do!" sang Lucy. "Rellard!"—a shout. "Rellardo, lardo, do! do! do!" She stepped high, weaving a pattern on the grass, stopping at important places to shout "Rellard!" and hold the cardboard figure level with her chin. "Rellardo, lardo," she chanted, bending to dangle the figure low, swinging, bobbing, stepping to the tune. "Rellardo, lardo, do! do! do!"

Shelley and Georgie joined in, with Lucy clapping, slapping their high-strutting knees, swinging, singing, "Rellardo, lardo, do! do! do!" over and over, until they reached the end, a joyous "Lardo!" Then they all fell laughing to the ground, arms and legs flung wide, the cardboard figure caught below Lucy's left ear.

And so Rellard became the name of the central figure in the drama they were creating.

"What's it mean, this Rellard?" Mum touched the cardboard medallion with her finger. "Who is he?"

"Oh, just somebody." Lucy shrugged.

"But who?"

Georgie looked up from his jam-laden piece of toast. "That's all that was left on that old toy theater you bought. R-E-L-L-A and another R and a D down at the end. So he's a Rellard."

"Oh, I see."

"He's a kind of king, isn't he, Luce?"

"Yes," agreed Lucy. "The Rellard has power. Power to do things!"

"If you say so." Mum laughed. "Salaam, kowtow, salaam, O Rellard!" and she made funny bows to the

7

Rellard hanging around Lucy's neck, which made Lucy giggle.

"We must have some adventures," Georgie declared. They were halfway through the summer holidays. "We've made so many plans for the Coronation of the Rellard that it's boring!"

Shelley paused in setting out a row of stones that marked the path to the throne and sat back on her heels.

"Adventures before the Coronation? What kind of adventures?"

"Maybe not adventures, exactly." Georgie's face struggled behind his smudged glasses. He tried to create an explanatory gesture but ended by putting his hands in his pockets and shrugging.

"Tests! We must have tests to prove that the one who is the Rellard is worthy!" Lucy's face paled with the force of her inspiration.

"Yes! Yes! Yes!" They knew at once that this was going to be a really good pretend and began immediately to invent the Trials.

Lucy insisted fiercely that the Trials had to be the same for all of them.

"But Lucy, you can't . . ." Shelley coaxed in her most reasonable tone but Lucy wouldn't let the words be said. When she was upset her face went white and her eyes blazed. She was upset now, clasping her withered right hand in the strong brown left one.

"The Trials have to be the same for all of us so that, when we pass through, whoever is the best is truly the Rellard. That's the only way to get the Power!"

Georgie and Shelley finally agreed.

And so the list of the Trials grew, Shelley and Georgie howling with laughter as they devised preposterous Trials, Lucy insisting that they must be serious, brushing aside their bubble of fun.

"The Trials must prepare one of us for the Power," she stated firmly and they could see that she was right. They worked at the list of deeds that made up each Trial, true testing deeds leading to the Power for the Rellard.

"What is the Power, anyway?" Georgie was lying on his back, speckled with sun and shade by the tree. "We keep talking about the Power, but what is it? What can it do?" He sat up.

Shelley was looking hard at him.

"It's all pretend, I know, but . . . well, if it *were* real, what would it be like?"

"It's a good Power," answered Lucy. "It curls around and makes the Rellard strong. That's the Power."

9

"What do you mean, curls around?"

And, surprising them both, Lucy produced a glass ball, nicked and pitted with age. Inside the solid sphere, lines of brilliant color swirled and spiraled, frozen in their turnings.

"Where did you get that?"

"I found it."

"Found it! Lucy, you took it! Where'd you take it from?"

"No! No! I didn't take it!"

"Lucy, I'll tell Mum!"

"No!" Lucy was close to tears. "I didn't take it! Please! I found it!"

"Where?"

"In the hole, the digging hole."

"What? What digging hole?" Georgie sat up straight.

"Over at the Jacobsen place."

At one time there had been a house on the large piece of empty land that backed onto their garden. It was gone now, only a treacherous hole remaining, cut out of the side of the sloping hill. The hole had been part of the rough limestone-lined cellar of the house. Over the years, sections of it had caved in and the derelict spot had been used as a small rubbish dump. Now it was a jungle of blackberry bushes, saplings and weeds, with an occasional jagged tooth of limestone showing. Everyone called it the Jacobsen place.

"Lucy, you know you're not supposed to go over there!"

"Did you get cut?" Georgie had been warned that cuts from old tin cans such as lurked in the shrubbery at the Jacobsen place could give a person a dreadful disease called lockjaw. He found the notion of being unable to open his jaws fascinating and sometimes practiced talking through clenched jaws, just in case he ever suffered such an injury.

"No, I didn't! I was just looking around and there was this loose dirt, already dug up, so I dug around too and found this. I knew straight away that it has power, because of the way it turns around inside, see?"

Indeed, in Lucy's hand, the glass ball with its captured spirals of color did seem to glow with a kind of power. They named it the Orb.

On another day, the air shrill with heat, the three children again rested under the tree.

Shelley picked at a scabby knee. "It's an awful long list of Trials. We can't do all of them, it will take too much time. Nobody'll get to be the Rellard before school starts."

"I suppose so." Georgie's face was lightly oiled with sweat. "We really don't need to do them all, just some of them."

"No!" Lucy sat erect, eyes stricken. "No! We can't! The Power won't come unless all the Trials are completed, every single one of them!"

"Come on, Luce." Georgie was getting fed up. He sat up slowly, rubbing his glasses on the front of his shirt. Spectacles finally settled on his nose again, he pushed them firmly into place with a fussy finger. "It's only a game. I can't even remember how many Trials there are."

"Twelve!" Lucy knelt, facing them. "There are twelve Trials. Then comes the Coronation, the handing over of the Orb and then," here she paused and took a deep breath, "then, the Rellard has the Power."

The children were caught in a moment of tense stillness, Lucy glaring fiercely at her brother and sister, eyes blazing, elbows stiff with passion.

Shelley gave in first. "All right, Lucy." Casually, Shelley looked down and brushed at her knee. "We'll do all twelve of the Trials. But when one of us wins and is the Rellard, well, then that will be the end of the game." Shelley stopped brushing at her knee and looked directly at her brother. "Okay, Georgie?"

"Sure! Yeah, okay!"

Speaking softly, Shelley leaned forward. "Okay, Luce?"

The shade flickered over Lucy's dark tangled hair. She was looking down, both hands in her lap.

"Lucy?" whispered Shelley. "Okay?"

Finally Lucy bobbed her head and whispered, "Yes."

They all felt a tremor of relief.

So in the time that was left to them, the Trials were a serious business. They decided to begin with the Trial of the Tree.

TWO

A Ceremony of Power

At the bottom of the small slope at the side of the house, astride the boundary between their place and the Carneys', towered a magnificent tree. It needed the three of them, arms stretched wide, to encircle the rough trunk. The thick bole rose straight to a great height before it began to branch. It was crowned with luxuriant foliage. It was a special tree, both for them and for the Carney boys. They all called it the Big Tree.

On their side of the Big Tree, an ancient, flat-bottomed punt had been settled among the roots and filled with sand. A yearly ritual was the filling of the punt with fresh sand, brought in Mr. Strachan's truck, from town.

The three of them reveled in the new sand. For a

time they would be occupied building roads, dams, and canals; making endless cakes and pies and sand cookies and, in preparation for the annual attack by the Carney boys, piling up a whole arsenal of sun-dried sandballs, heaped on the stern of the punt ready for throwing.

As summer wore on, the sand in the punt began to lose its fresh golden color, and gradually the pile would pack down until, in winter, it made only an insignificant mound under the snow. After the spring thaw, the punt would hold a small packed puddle of sand and Dad would ring up Mr. Strachan for a new load.

Close to the sand-filled punt and still under the sweep of the Big Tree stood the pump. When Dad was a little boy, big pipes had been laid in a deep trench across the backyard and water brought to the house, so the pump wasn't needed. But Grandma had told them to leave it where it was. It still brought up stinging cold water from the deep well—water they used for their sandpies, water to fill their meandering canals and rivers, water to drink, and water to wash the heat of the summer from their faces.

One branch of the Big Tree grew straight out over the border between the two properties and from it hung the swing, which was an old tire turned inside out and cut away at the sides and top. The families took turns replacing the rope as it frayed and raveled with use. At least one yearly battle was fought with the Carneys over the use or misuse of the swing.

"The first Trial will be to climb the Big Tree," Shelley announced. So imposing was its presence in their lives that Georgie and Lucy immediately concurred. They knew that it was exactly the place to begin the Trials.

Shelley was voted the scribe and put in charge of writing down all the rules of the Trials as well as a report. Mother provided them with a brown notebook that was originally intended as a recipe book but ended up at the back of the silverware drawer.

Shelley read as she wrote. "The rules are . . . Number One. The contestant for the Trial of the Tree is not allowed to use any helps such as a ladder or a rope."

"Or spikes," Georgie interrupted.

"Spikes? Do you have spikes?"

"No," said Georgie, "but put it in anyway. Spikes would be a real help."

". . . or spikes," continued Shelley. "Rule Number Two. The contestant must climb all the way to the top of the Big Tree and wave his or her banner to signal that he or she has reached said top."

"Said top?" Lucy asked. "Do we have to say 'top' when we get there?"

"It's a kind of report language," explained Shelley. "You don't have to say anything." She continued to write. "The other two contestants can then verify that the first contestant has truly reached the top of the Big Tree. Rule Number Thr . . ."

"Not from here we can't."

"Georgie, stop interrupting!"

"But we can't verify, not from here."

"He's right." Lucy pointed. "You can't see the top of the Big Tree from here. We're too under it."

They turned to look up at the Big Tree, hugely green against the sky. Shelley stood up and eyed their house, turning her head as she measured it against the height of the tree.

"If we were up on the sunroom roof, we would be about even with the top of the Big Tree," she pointed out.

Georgie and Lucy could see that this was true and Rule Number Two had a subsection that stated that the two contestants not climbing the tree would watch from the roof of the sunroom.

"Monitor, put 'monitor the climb' instead of 'watch the climb,' " insisted Georgie. "It sounds better for rules."

"We'll have to do the Trial on Thursday," commented Lucy. That was their mother's golf day and they always saved any faintly dangerous undertaking for Thursday. "That way she won't worry," Lucy added.

"Rule Number Three. The contestant must climb down the tree. Whoever does all of the above, in the fastest time as timed by the stopwatch, wins the Trial of the Tree." Shelley snapped shut the notebook.

Georgie patted the knobbed watch that swung from his neck on a shoelace. "Timing it exactly like that, it makes the Trial scientific."

"Banners! Let's get our banners ready now!" Lucy raced across the lawn ahead of Shelley and Georgie.

"Shell, about Lucy . . ." Georgie clicked the knobs of the watch in and out.

"Stop that. You'll break it."

"No, I won't." Georgie stopped fiddling with the watch and faced Shelley. "Lucy, what if she falls and hurts herself because of her . . . because of . . ."

"She's better now." Shelley tucked the notebook under her arm. "And she's stubborn. She wants to do it."

"Yes, I know . . . but still, she's different, somehow. Since we started this Rellard thing . . . oh, I don't know." Georgie went back to clicking the stopwatch knobs.

"Georgie, she wants to win. She wants to prove something . . . that she *is* okay, I guess. She wants it really badly, so we have to go through with it, to help her."

"But what if she slips and falls and breaks something? It's hard enough to climb that old tree with two good hands."

"She'll be all right."

"Should we maybe . . . well, *let* her win?"

"It has to be fair and square, Georgie. Otherwise Lucy will never get over this Rellard business. If she loses, she loses fair and square. Same if she wins."

"But she can't win! Not with her weak arm!" Georgie frowned and rubbed his ear. "It doesn't seem fair."

"Hey! Look at my banner!" yelled Lucy from the upstairs hall window. "Isn't it beautiful?"

And to her brother and sister looking up from the lawn below, Lucy seemed to be enwreathed in a swirl of shimmering rosy light as she learned far out the window and waved a red silk scarf.

Thursday arrived and their mother went to play golf, leaving Shelley in charge. All of the Carneys, except for Carrie—the oldest and quietest—were up at the Lakes for a week, and the Big Tree stood quietly at the bottom of the backyard.

They drew straws and Georgie went first.

"Don't mess up the watch," he admonished Shelley. "You have to give a real hard push to the stop knob, otherwise it won't work."

"Don't worry!"

"Go on, Georgie! Good luck and good fortune to you!" Lucy trailed her banner around her brother's shoulders in a ritualistic gesture. She ended with a flourish of her red silk square, a bright salute.

Georgie flicked his own blue-and-white-checked scarf in acknowledgment, turned, and walked slowly across the lawn to the Big Tree.

"Don't start climbing until we yell ready!" The girls raced into the house and up the stairs to the bathroom, where they scrambled out onto the sunroom roof. They were almost on the same level as the top of the huge tree. At its foot, they could see Georgie, banner trailing.

"Okay, go!" yelled Shelley, pressing the start button on the watch.

"Go! Go! Go!" Lucy yelled, swirling her banner in bright curves and dips.

Georgie tucked his banner inside the waist of his shorts and began to climb. The hardest part was the trunk, but the knobs and burls that the old tree had accumulated over the years provided some finger- and toeholds. By stretching one arm very long while standing on a high burl, Georgie was able to grasp the first branch and pull himself up onto it. After that it was fairly easy.

It was eerie inside the foliage of the tree. The leaves spoke in soft rustlings. The branches squeaked and creaked as they swayed. The light was thick and green.

As he approached the top of the tree Georgie concentrated on judging the weight-bearing quality of each branch. When one sagged or swayed danger- ously, he would back down and search out a stronger branch. His hands grew slippery and he wouldn't let himself look down.

Finally he emerged from the dense foliage and could see the house and the two girls on the roof. It was a bit of a struggle getting his banner out of his shorts. It had slipped around the back during the climb. But finally he was able to wave it and re- ceived an answering flourish and cheer from the girls. Then it was down, carefully but quickly. He skinned his arm a bit on the last slide down the trunk but was able to throw the other up in a trium- phant gesture when he finally stood on the ground.

He was astonished to find that it had taken him nine minutes and forty-two seconds to climb the Big Tree.

"You're crazy! I went fast! You must have pushed the wrong button!"

"Right. Do it again and we'll compare," snapped Shelley.

Georgie knew that he couldn't climb that tree again, not today, anyway, so he fumed and muttered and let himself be persuaded to time Shelley's climb, which was next.

Shelley's yellow banner was brandished from the top of the Big Tree in short order. However, her descent was marked by the loud crack of a breaking branch, and it was quite a few minutes before she lowered herself, pale and shaken, to the ground and gave a cursory wigwag of her banner.

"Ten minutes, fifty-five seconds," chortled Georgie to himself.

Lucy hopped impatiently from foot to foot, waiting at the foot of the tree as Shelley walked back to the house.

"You okay?" asked Georgie as Shelley crept carefully through the window.

"Yes. Fine. Great climb." Shelley's offhand manner didn't fool Georgie.

"Took you nine minutes fifty-five seconds." He

generously lopped off a whole minute to make up for the scary fall she had climbing through the heavy green of the tree.

Shelley threw him a sideways glance of suspicion. Georgie concentrated on the knobs of the watch. Then both of them focused their attention on the impatient figure of Lucy, poised for her climb.

"Ready," called Georgie, dragging out the word so that it sounded like the call of a horn. "Ready—ready—reaa-a-a-de-e-e-e-e!" His call seemed to find an echo in the tree. "Go!"

Lucy appeared to leap up the trunk of the tree, banner high in her hand. The bright red flickered up through the foliage, faster and faster, and was thrust triumphantly through to the sunlight above the tree, a scarlet salute to the sky in Lucy's right hand.

At that moment, as the luminous red banner broke free of the green of the tree and blazoned itself against the sky, in that bright long moment, the whole of the Big Tree began to move. To the two children perched on the sunroom roof, it looked as if the tree were dancing.

"Hey, look!" Georgie gasped. Shelley could only stare, speechless. But then the moment was past and now it was only the tree's leaves, rustling in a newly sprung breeze.

Down, down through the greenly busy leaves descended Lucy, quickly, neatly, skillfully. Branches seemed to spring to her feet, were ready under her hands. Down and down fluttered the red banner and Lucy until they landed with a swirl at the base of the trunk. Golden sand scuffed up around Lucy's sneakers.

"Yes!" yelled Lucy, and threw up both arms.

"Four minutes!" Georgie couldn't believe his eyes. "Four minutes! Hey, Luce! You did it in four minutes! Hey! How about that!" and he capered on the roof, laughing at the delightfulness of it all. "Wow! Four minutes!"

And so it went, through all the other Trials. The Trial of Water, the Trial of the Diggings, the Trial of the Dark Night, all of them, all twelve of the Trials —all were lost by Shelley and Georgie, lost to Lucy. In the end, Lucy won all the Trials, all twelve of them, fair and square.

Today they had crowned her the Rellard and she had received the Power.

At the Coronation, Georgie held up the iron circlet in disgust.

"Where did you find this? The digging hole again?"

"It's a crown. It's *my* Crown."

"Okay, Lucy, but don't blame me if you get lock-jaw or something."

Then Georgie spoke the Coronation words that Lucy had made him write down on a bit of paper so that he wouldn't forget.

"I crown you Rellard," he intoned, "Keeper of the Power. The Power of the Water, the Power of the Fire, the Power of the Leaf and the Rock, of the Wing and Claw and Feather. Use them well, O Rellard."

He lowered the rough iron circlet onto Lucy's head, where it fitted exactly.

Shelley knelt and presented the faded pillow that made a nest for the Orb.

"I bestow upon you, O Rellard, the Power."

Lucy picked up the glass ball in both hands, raising it so that she was looking directly into the swirling spirals of color.

"The Power is here," she whispered.

Carefully, she took one hand away, leaving the other still holding the glass ball high. Then she began to lower the Orb, slowly and carefully. The hand holding the Orb, the withered hand, trembled, for the Orb was solid and heavy. But the hand held steady and firm beneath the spiraled ball. Finally, she rested the hand in her lap.

"I want to be alone, please," Lucy the Rellard requested in a husky voice.

Shelley and Georgie walked around the shed, up to the house where they sat on the front step.

"She really believes, Shelley. She thinks she has some sort of power. It's not a game for her."

"I don't think it ever was a game for her. It was always real."

"Do you think she really has a power?"

"I don't know."

"What do we do now?"

"Nothing. It's all over."

"Yes. I guess so, Shelley. I guess it's all over."

The two children sat quietly, waiting.

THREE

Forging a Talisman

"You can't be playing that Rellard game today, there's too much to do," announced their mother at breakfast the next morning. Puffs of flour rose as she kneaded away at the bread she was baking for the annual trip to the Lakes.

"It's all over now, anyway." Shelley sedately spooned up her cereal. "Isn't it, Georgie?"

Georgie grunted from behind his comic.

"Well, it certainly kept you busy for a while." Mum dusted more flour onto the board and began her rhythmic pushing and turning of the dough. "Who became the Rellard in the end?" Her voice was casual.

"Lucy did." Georgie expertly flicked over a page of his comic book without putting down his spoon.

"Oh?" The pushing and turning stopped, momentarily, then continued. "Well, that's terrific! Congratulations, dear."

Lucy sipped her milk, eyes steady over the rim of the glass.

"What does it mean to be a Rellard?" The dough was getting harder to knead, bulging stiffly against Mum's knuckles.

Lucy set down her glass. "The Rellard has the Power," she said.

"Oh?" Mum turned the smooth lump of dough into a bowl. "What kind of power?"

"I don't know," answered Lucy.

"Maybe she can fly!" laughed Georgie. "You sure looked like you were flying when you went up the Big Tree, Lucy. Wow! Four minutes!"

"What tree?" Their mother paused in her scraping of the breadboard, bits of dough in her hand.

"Oh, just that old tree," Shelley answered, darting a warning look at her brother.

"I'll have to learn the Power." Lucy swirled her spoon around in her cereal. "Maybe I can learn to fly."

"Lucy, don't play with your food." Mum moved to the sink.

"Lucy, the game is over now," hissed Shelley.

"You're the Rellard but we aren't playing that game anymore."

"I know that." Lucy's eyes were serious. "But now I must find out myself about the Power. That won't be a game."

"I told you so," muttered Georgie.

Shelley felt helpless, caught in the direct gaze of her sister's eyes. She knew it was all a game that they had made up and yet . . .

"Don't worry, Shelley. All will be well." Lucy smiled as she spoke and Shelley felt unaccountably relieved.

"All is not well, my fine feathered friends," announced Mum, clattering back to the table. "We're supposed to be packed and ready to leave for the Lakes by three o'clock and so far nothing, *nothing* in the way of packing has been accomplished! So get moving, all of you." They moved, but in a moment Lucy was back.

"Can I have these?" She pointed at the small pile of leftover dough pieces.

"Sure. Fine." Mum was pulling thermoses and plastic boxes out of a low cupboard, piling them on the counter.

"Thanks." Lucy hurried away, hands cupped carefully around the fragments of dough. In their

29

bedroom neat piles of clothing covered Shelley's bed. She was contemplating a pair of blue sneakers when Lucy came in.

"Do you think I should take these?"

"Sure." Lucy cleared a space on her desk and began to knead the dough scraps into a little ball.

"I've already put in the red sneakers and my white moccasins and the sandals."

"Take them. They match your new jeans."

"Yes, I know. But I've got so much in my case now . . ."

"Put them in mine."

Lucy's withered hand held the ball of dough steady, while with her left hand she manipulated the dough, pinching out legs and arms and a head. She hummed a little song softly as she worked, tongue caught between her teeth, shoulders hunched. Before the sickness had withered her arm and hand, Lucy had been right-handed. It took a lot of concentration to make her awkward left hand do the work of the right.

"Thanks, Luce. Hey! Is this all you're taking?" Shelley peered into Lucy's open suitcase.

"Does he look like a man?" She held up the dough.

"Sort of." Shelley bent over the case again. "Lucy, you have to take more than one pair of shorts for two weeks. *And* one T-shirt, *and* . . ." Shelley energetically rummaged through Lucy's case with one hand, blue sneakers held aloft in the other.

"Leave my stuff alone!" Lucy slammed down the lid of the case.

Shelley glared, plonked the sneakers on the closed lid, and went back to the neatly sorted arrangement of clothing on her bed.

Lucy worked a while longer on the little dough figure. She stood looking at it for a long moment, then went to Shelley's dressing table and began poking in the open jewelry box there.

"What *are* you doing? You know not to mess with my things!" Shelley whisked the box out from under Lucy's tentative finger.

"I just need a little bead or sequin or something."

"What for?"

"It has to be a part of something you've worn and liked," Lucy instructed. "And small."

"What are you going to do with it?"

"Put it in my little Rellard man. From me I'm putting in the little blue stone that fell out of the ring from my Captain Marvel kit."

"Lucy, forget about that Rellard business," pleaded Shelley.

"I'll get something from Georgie, too. Then he'll be a part of all three of us."

Shelley clutched the jewelry box to her chest.

"Please, Shelley? It's just a little dough Rellard. That cardboard one I had wore out."

Shelley set the box on the table and began to go through its tiny drawers. Finally she held up a small object. "You can have this," she said, and she dropped it into Lucy's waiting palm. It was an ivory bead, carved in the shape of a flower. The tiny blossom was tinted a pale rose.

"Oh, Shell, how beautiful! Thank you." Lucy reached up to plant a swift kiss on the older girl's cheek. Shelley flushed happily and went back to her packing, humming to herself.

Lucy pocketed the bead, cautiously picked up the little dough man, and went in search of Georgie. His bedroom door was locked with a "Keep Out, This Means You" sign dangling from the knob.

"Georgie, let me in!" yelled Lucy, giving the door a tentative kick.

Noises from the other side of the door stopped.

"Go away. You can read."

"Please, Georgie," pleaded Lucy. "It's important."

"Say the password."

"How can I say the password when I don't *know* the password? What are you up to now?"

"Food. It's some kind of food. Go on, guess."

Georgie was standing right up against the inside of the door.

Lucy frowned. "Bread?"

"No. Further down the alphabet. Guess again!"

"Custard? Doughnut?" Lucy began to hop up and down. "Georgie, I'll never guess the stupid password, let me in please, it's important!"

"Fried rice!" Georgie yanked the door open triumphantly. "You were almost there."

"That's two words, not one. How can it be a pass*word?* You should have said pass*words,* then I would have got it."

"Forget it." Georgie began to close the door.

"No, no! Fried rice, please, Georgie! Fried rice!"

"Okay, you can come in."

Georgie's room was full of things. Airplanes dived on lengths of fishing line from the ceiling. Model cars, trucks, and war machines competed for every little flat space with jars of shells, boxes of rocks, bundles of papers, stacks and stacks of comics, and little piles of assorted objects. The shelves along one side of the room were absolutely jam-packed—maps, more models, dioramas, art projects, books, more comics, empty jars, jars full of screws, nails, rocks, all carefully sorted—a long line of telephone insulators, packets of seeds, games, old toys, matchbooks, clocks in various states of disassembly, even an old dismantled radio. A target, stuffed but rapidly coming unstuffed, stood against the wall, and darts, arrows, and a spear were sticking out of it. A red sock was hanging from the end of the spear. There was an aquarium, an ant farm, and a worm farm. Gazing from the top of the bookshelves was a slightly cross-eyed stuffed owl, wings outstretched, ready to take off.

"What do you want?" demanded Georgie. "I'm busy packing."

"Some little thing of yours to put on him." Lucy held up the dough man.

"What kind of little thing? What *is* he, anyway?"

"He's a Rellard man and something you like and have touched."

"I thought we'd finished with that Rellard business."

"I need something from you and I have a bead from Shelley and I'll put in something from me—this little blue stone, see?—and he'll be like a remembrance of it all. Just a little Rellard man."

"Let's see. . . ." Georgie frowned slightly as he turned to consider his possessions. "Some little thing . . ." He shifted a jar of stones and shells and riffled through a pack of dog-eared football cards. Then he moved to the shelf that held a collection of clocks in pieces and began poking and pushing with an inquis-

itive finger in a box that had a broken corner. "No
. . . not that . . . no . . . maybe . . ." He held
something in his hand a moment. Then, "Nope,
might need that," and he dropped it back into the
box.

"Georgie! Hurry!" Lucy was shifting from one
foot to the other.

Georgie rummaged for a moment longer, muttering and nodding. Suddenly his fingers pounced and
drew from the collapsing box a piece of bright
golden metal.

"How about this?" he asked, holding it out to
Lucy. "This was my good-luck piece for a while. It's
shaped kind of like a little crown. See?"

"That's perfect, Georgie! Perfect! Thank you."
Lucy made a deep bow to her brother. "Thank you,
O great brother Georgie," she intoned in a deep
voice, making another low bow.

Georgie laughed. "Go on, get out of here. I have
to pack."

Lucy scampered down the stairs, through the
house, and out to the lean-to behind the shed. She
moved the old cane chair from its position and
struggled to lift the large flat rock that the chair had
concealed. Beneath the rock, soil had been dug out,
and resting in the hollow, cushioned in a nest of
leaves, were the Orb and the Crown. Lucy lifted the

two objects carefully from the cavity and set them on the ground before her. She placed the Crown on her head. Next to the Orb she put the little dough man, his head pointing toward the glass ball.

"Now," whispered Lucy to herself, and from her pocket she drew the flower bead, the bright metal crown, and the blue stone. Carefully she pressed the bit of metal on the head of the figure.

"That's your crown, Rellard man. It does look like a crown, too," she murmured. The flower bead was pressed into the dough man's tummy. "Your heart," Lucy said. In the right hand of the figure she pressed the blue stone. "The Power," she muttered.

She sat quietly, regarding the little dough figure, with its golden crown at a rakish angle, its flowery belly button and lumpy right hand holding the blue stone.

She picked up the Orb and held it in her right hand above the figure.

"Power of the Fire and Water, the Leaf and Rock, the Wing, the Claw and Feather . . . enter this little man," she intoned, and the spirals of color in the glass ball began to move, slowly at first, then faster and faster, until the Orb was glowing brightly. Lucy's hand trembled but held firm as the light of the Orb fell on the little dough man and he began to bake. His doughy arms and legs grew smooth, firm and round, lightly browning. The soft mass hardened and the metal and bead and stone warmed also as they were firmly cooked into the figure. Lucy began to lower the glass ball. "It is done. It is done," she whispered. The swirls of color slowed, the light faded, and when the ball was resting on the ground once again, its colored spirals were stopped in their turnings.

"Whew," breathed Lucy. "Hard work!" Quickly she returned the glass ball and the crown to their hiding place. She carefully strung a shoelace through the holes she'd left in the little golden brown figure and tied it around her neck.

"I'll color you on the way to the Lakes," she promised, slipping the dough man under her shirt. She ran into the house to finish her packing.

FOUR

The Power Revealed

The Lakes was really one big body of water, but it had such an irregular shoreline and so many islands dotted throughout that it seemed to be many small lakes strung together.

The family had inherited their old cottage at the Lakes from one of Mother's aunts. It crouched sleepily beneath tall trees, up to its eaves in shrubs, peering myopically down the short hill to the dock and the stretch of lake below. The cottage was old and mossy and smelled of the damp, but every summer it seemed to rouse itself from its dream and welcome the family for their annual visit.

The cottage was on the quiet side of the Lakes—the side away from the marina, the shops, and the tall white houses that were two stories high and filled with tourists. Occasionally, Georgie or Shelley or Lucy would see a water-skier, swooping through rainbowed arcs of spray, or a sailboat gliding smoothly behind an island. Once during their stay the whole family would visit the Palisades Amusement Park, ride the roller coaster and the zipper and the bumper cars, stumble laughing through the funhouse, and become part of the noisy, raucous crowd that peopled the other side of the Lakes.

At times, Shelley yearned to be more a part of the busy life on the other side. Georgie was absolutely contented with the quiet old cottage and its surrounding woods. He spent the whole two weeks tracking, trapping, netting, hooking, or in any way possible capturing the small creatures and insects that populated the woods and their bit of the lake.

Lucy loved the cottage. She wrapped herself in the remnants of its dream and played out long solitary dramas on the dim front porch or out under the trees. The only thing she didn't like were the bugs. Flying bugs that thumped the screens at night, creeping bugs that feathered across her hand in the dark—she dreaded all the insects that inhabited the old cottage and especially detested the snarling mosquitoes. On poor Lucy their bites swelled and itched ferociously, almost making her weep.

"I think I'll try the Power out on the bugs," she announced, standing at the bottom of the flight of stone steps that led up to the cottage. They had all had to carry something up from the car, and Lucy was resting before the long climb.

"That's fine with me," said Mum, as she pushed by, loaded with blankets and sheets. "But do it after you carry that stuff up."

At last the car was unloaded. Lucy went to stand on a little knob of ground that reared up at the back of the cottage, just to one side of the derelict chicken house.

She stood with her good hand resting on her hip, carefully surveying the cottage, the overgrown garden, the stone steps staggering down the hill, the lake below, and the dock basking in the late afternoon sun. It was very still and a cloud of midges shivered in the air between her and the house.

She reached into the neck of her shirt and pulled out the Rellard man. She cradled it in both hands, close to her chin, and blew gently. The little figure began to glow. The crown took on a dazzle of gold and the flowery navel bloomed. The blue stone in the right hand blazed.

"You are my messenger," she intoned. "You are

my bug messenger." She continued to blow on the figure. The colors she had inked onto the baked dough during the long drive up to the Lakes brightened. She had given the Rellard man a purple cloak and yellow shoes. He had two bright blue eyes beneath his crown.

"Go to all the bugs who live around this cottage," she ordered, "and tell them to stay away. They must stay away until I tell them to return. Tell them, O bug messenger! It is my command!"

Again she blew on the medallion, cupped it in her right hand, and raised it high above her head. Intoning "Go, bug messenger, go, bug messenger," she turned slowly, carefully shifting her feet on the little mound. When she completed her turn and faced the cottage once again, she lowered the medallion.

All was quiet. The little quivering cloud of midges had disappeared.

Lucy pulled the shoelace over her head and pushed the medallion down the neck of her shirt.

"I am the Rellard, with the Power of the Wing and Claw and Feather," she sang as she tramped down the path to the back door of the house.

"Well, I got rid of all those awful bugs," she announced to her mother.

"Did you, darling?"

Lucy knew it wasn't a real question and went to unpack her suitcase.

"I just can't understand it!"

"Understand what?"

Georgie was drifting about, butterfly net in hand. A row of empty jars was lined up on the bottom step of the porch. Dad was rocking in the hammock, leg draped over one side, lazily pushing himself back and forth. Georgie stopped beside the hammock.

"I can't understand where all the insects and things are."

"Hunting not so good these days, eh?" Dad reached out and lightly punched Georgie's stomach.

"Usually I've caught lots of things by now. It's been two days and there's nothing. No butterflies, no caterpillars, no dragonflies! Not even any ordinary flies."

Dad sat up and put both feet on the ground, stopping the hammock's swing.

"You're right, now that I come to think of it. I haven't seen any flies at all this year. As for the other things, are you sure you haven't lost your touch?"

Georgie didn't even deign to answer. He was an expert bug catcher. "There just don't seem to be any insects about," he said finally, and fiddled with his net. "The birds are gone, too."

"Really?" Dad sat up even straighter. "I wonder if someone has been spraying poison around here. Let's have a scout around."

They searched carefully, checking the trees and under the bushes, moving in ever-widening circles around the cottage. They could hear Lucy singing before they finally came upon her. She was kneeling in a circle of stones.

"Rowan, Rowan. Vay, vay, vay, O, Rowan, ishti vay Rowan," she sang.

"Be sure to wash your hands before you eat, young lady," ordered Dad. "Those stones could be covered with insecticide." He tramped on.

"What's he mean?" Her humlike song interrupted, Lucy sat back on her heels and questioned her brother.

"He thinks someone has sprayed poison around here."

"Oh, no!"

"Yes! And that could be what's killed off all the insects and things." Georgie finished tucking his shirt into his shorts and tramped off after his father.

"Georgie!"

"What?" He stopped and half turned toward Lucy.

"Georgie, I sent them away with the Power."

"Oh, Lucy, don't be silly." He turned to follow his father.

Lucy watched them disappear. "I *did* send them away, Georgie! I did!" she called out. Then she resumed her song. "Rowan, O Rowan, vay, vay, Rowan O Rowan O," she droned, intent in her circle of stones.

At dinner that night Dad and Georgie were full of their discovery.

"There's not an insect on the property," Dad declared. "At least not one that we could see or hear."

"How strange." Their mother was slicing a new loaf of bread.

"And Mum, have you noticed the birds? They're gone, too. There's nothing for them to eat." Georgie blinked importantly behind his crooked glasses.

"Now that you mention it, I have missed the songs of the birds."

Shelley spoke up. "The dragonflies must be gone too. Usually there's a lot of them around the dock but there weren't any today."

"Shelley, you shouldn't have spent so much time on the dock today. You look like you have very bad sunburn!"

"I'm okay."

"I sent them away," announced Lucy.

"Well, you don't look fine to me. Too much sun can make you very sick, you know that!"

"Mum, I'm fine!"

"It's an ecological disaster!" Georgie was redly indignant. "You all don't seem to appreciate that. It's an ecological disaster!"

"I wonder who I should phone to see if there has been any spraying done around here?" mused Dad. "It would be trespassing, because I haven't ever asked anyone to do any spraying."

"I sent the bugs away," repeated Lucy, a little louder.

"I don't know who to call, dear. Shelley, I want you to go have a wash in cool water and I'll come put something on your sunburn. You look feverish to me. Too much sun can give you a fever, you know that."

"Maybe the local council would know." Dad pushed his chair away from the table.

"I don't like mosquitoes so I sent the insects away," insisted Lucy.

"I don't know, dear. Now, Shelley, I mean it. You pop straight into bed while I hunt for the thermometer."

"You come with me," growled Shelley, clamping Lucy's wrist in a hot hand and dragging her out to the veranda where they slept.

They left Georgie and Dad still talking.

"Mum, I think we should report it. After all, you should report an ecological disaster, shouldn't you? Mum?" But their mother was engrossed in her search. "Dad?"

"Yes, Georgie! I'll ring someone when I've worked out who to call! Now we should really write down . . ."

"*What* have you done?" Shelley's eyes were red from her long afternoon in the sun and that added to her look of ferocity. Lucy shrank back and tried to free her arm.

"I just sent them away."

"Who away?"

"The insects. All those awful bugs!"

"What!" Shelley dropped Lucy's wrist in amazement.

"Yes, especially the mosquitoes. I hate those mosquitoes!"

"Lucy, what did you do with them?"

"I sent them away until I tell them to come back. You don't look very well, Shelley. You should go to bed."

"Lucy, *how* did you send the bugs away?"

"I'll get you a glass of water. You want a glass of water?"

They could hear their mother's footsteps, coming through the cottage.

"Lucy," gasped Shelley desperately. "Lucy, how did you do it?"

"With the Power of the Rellard, Shelley. I told you I had to learn about it."

"Oh, Lucy." Shelley sank down onto her bed and began to rock. She hugged herself and shivered as she rocked. "Oh, Lucy," she groaned.

"I told you not to try to get a suntan in one day, Shelley, and look at you now! You've made yourself sick." Mum sent Lucy to get some baking soda and began to undress the shivering, moaning girl. "Oh, Shelley, love, why did you stay in the sun so long?"

"Oh, Mum," moaned Shelley, "what am I going to do?"

"There, there," soothed her mother. "It's only a bad sunburn."

The next day Shelley was too sick to get up.

"Just leave her alone, everybody, and let her sleep," ordered Mum.

"No," pleaded Shelley. "Please, I want Lucy."

"Well, just for a little while and then you must sleep. You've got a temperature." Mum went out to the kitchen.

"Lucy," whispered Shelley, voice hoarse with urgency, "you mustn't tell them about the insects, about sending them away."

"Why not? Anyway, I already told them but they don't listen. You're the only one who heard me."

"I know. I think it would be . . . well . . . might not be a good thing if they did hear you."

Lucy just sat and looked at her sister.

"I don't know why, but please, don't tell anyone," insisted Shelley.

Lucy sat quietly for a long moment and then nodded. "Okay. I won't." She leaned forward, smiling. "Shelley, I think I could make you well now, the same way I sent the bugs away."

"Lucy!"

"I know I can, Shell," and Lucy began to draw the dough man out of the front of her shirt.

Shelley shrank back against the pillow. "No, Lucy. Please. I'm afraid!"

"But it's a good power. I told you. It can't hurt you."

"Lucy, put that away. Don't!"

Lucy took a long look at her sister and slipped the medallion back. "I'm sorry, Shelley. I didn't mean to make you cry."

"Don't tell anyone else about the Power and the insects. Promise!" Shelley leaned forward, fiercely determined.

"I promise."

Their mother appeared at the door, a jug of water in one hand.

"Out you go now, Lucy, and let your sister get some rest." She began to close the canvas blinds, shutting out the sun and filling the veranda with a green twilight.

Lucy looked back at the girl in the bed.

"Promise?" mouthed Shelley silently.

Lucy nodded and kissed her hand to Shelley. Then she dashed through the cottage, hurrying to find her father and her brother. They ignored her when she ran up, but she trailed along after them anyway as they continued their search for insects. The three of them pushed their way through thick underbrush until they came to the sagging barbed wire that marked the edge of their property. On the other side lay an open field, sloping down to the lake on the right and ruffled with tall trees on the top and far side.

"Will you look at that?" breathed Dad.

They stood and looked and listened.

The warm sunlight that danced above the heavy-headed grasses was alive with insects. Dragonflies darted and danced, flashing iridescent signals to the heavy bees that bumbled head-first into the wild blossoms hidden below. Clouds of midges shivered, collapsed, and reappeared in another place. Crickets chirred and grasshoppers leaped and spat. Birds were swooping from the trees, their songs an airy obbligato to the steady insect thrum that filled the air above the field.

"There they are!" Georgie waved his arm. "All over there! But why not here?"

"Why not, indeed." Dad pulled at his ear. "I just can't understand it!"

"We don't need all those creepy bugs," asserted Lucy.

"It's terrible," said Georgie as he turned and faced into their own woods. "Look at that. Dead! Dead as a doornail!"

"No! Not dead!" Lucy protested.

"Look at it," Georgie ordered. "It sure looks dead to me!"

And when she looked, it looked dead to Lucy, too. The sunlight fell in shafts through the trees but no midges danced golden in the light. It was a still, silent wood that greeted them and Lucy was thoughtful as they walked back to the cottage. Her father went off to consult with a neighbor about the suspected spraying of poison and Georgie trailed down to the dock with his fishing rod.

Lucy sought out her mother. She threw her arms around her mother's neck, breathing in the lovely scent of her cheek.

"Why did the birds go?"

"M-m-m-m-m?"

"Why did the birds go away? Can't they stay even if the bugs are all gone?"

"They would be hungry then. They eat the insects."

"Can't they eat seeds or something? Parakeets do."

"Well, yes, but that wouldn't be enough. It's all to do with the balance of nature."

"What's that?"

"It's about one thing depending on another to live." Mother smoothed back Lucy's hair. "Now run along to the kitchen. I've left your sandwich on the table." She opened her book.

Lucy chewed over the balance of nature with her sandwich. She knew what nature was because they had made a nature table in the second grade and Lucy had brought leaves and moss and bark to make a tree on the bulletin board behind the table.

Balance she knew from when she and her friend Judy played balance on the seesaws at the playground. That was before Jamie Patterson lost his two front teeth by getting hit on the chin with a seesaw and they were taken away. But when the brightly painted seesaw boards were there, all up and down over the round pipes, Lucy and Judy sat on opposite ends of one board, lifting their feet slowly, keeping the board even. Judy would move in a bit toward the middle because she was bigger than Lucy. When it was in good balance with their feet down, they would slowly raise their legs and stretch them straight out in front on the board. They became very good at balancing and could keep the seesaw straight for quite a long time, doing fine adjustments to the balance with their arms and bodies. At times, they kept the balance just by varying the amount of breath they drew into their lungs.

So, Lucy reasoned, this balance of nature her mother was talking about must be a keeping of the things of nature even, and somehow her making the insects go away had caused the balance to be upset, just the way one end of the seesaw would crash to the ground when she or Judy moved and shifted the balance.

Lucy sighed. She really had enjoyed these few days without the mosquitoes and their painful bites. She had been able to play under the old cottage and explore the chicken-run without fear of spiders or other bugs dropping in her hair or darting up her arm or over her foot.

She went along to the sleeping porch. Shelley was asleep, face flushed and sweaty, breathing little snores into the cool green light.

"Good thing I got rid of the flies. They would be buzzing like mad now on the blinds, bothering Shelley," thought Lucy.

Shelley gave a little moan. Lucy could see the throb of pulse in the older girl's throat. It fluttered quickly beneath the flushed skin of her neck.

Lucy stood considering her sister and then made up her mind.

"I'll make her better, anyway. She looks pretty sick." She drew out the medallion and blew gently on it as before. The little dough man began to glow.

"Make Shelley better," crooned Lucy, dangling the medallion on its shoelace over her sleeping sister. She dangled the medallion up over Shelley's whole body, stopping at her head.

"Send the Power through her and take away the hotness. Make Shelley well."

Slipping the dough man back under her shirt, Lucy knelt beside the bed, chin on folded arms, face close to Shelley's right ear. She watched the quick flutter of pulse in Shelley's neck. It began to slow, throbbing steadily and with more power. The red flush on Shelley's face and neck and arms cooled. Shelley sighed, a relieved sigh. She opened her eyes and looked up at the ceiling.

"Hi, Shell," breathed Lucy.

Shelley turned her head and looked at her sister. They were so close their noses were almost touching. Shelley's eyes were clear.

"Hi, Lucy."

"Feeling better?"

Shelley blinked her eyes and considered. "Yes. I do feel better."

Lucy looked smug.

Shelley narrowed her eyes. "What have you done?"

Lucy giggled.

Shelley sat up, indignation ruffling her hair. "You did it, didn't you?" she accused.

Lucy grinned.

"You used the Power on me! That's not fair! I asked you not to. You could have made me disappear, like the insects!"

"You looked awful lying there." Lucy sat back on her heels. "Besides, I told you it was a good power."

"Tell that to the bugs!" stormed Shelley.

"I need you." Lucy looked ready to cry. "I

wouldn't hurt you, Shell."

Shelley lay down again. "I can't believe it," she told the ceiling. "She really does have a power."

"I have it but I could do with some help," sniffed Lucy.

"You need help when you've got all this power?"

"I need advice, Shelley. I really messed up with the bugs and I don't know what to do." Lucy went on to explain what she had worked out about the insects and the balance of nature and the birds being gone and the seesaw crashing to the ground.

"There's only one thing to do," announced Shelley as she pulled her T-shirt over her head. "You'll have to tell the insects to come back."

"All of them?"

"What do you mean, all of them? Of course! All of them!"

"But couldn't I tell the mosquitoes to stay away? They always bite me so much; they don't bite you or Georgie nearly so much but they really hurt me. Couldn't I make them stay away if I let all the others come back?" Lucy was almost in tears.

Shelley paused. "I don't know, Lucy. Maybe you could." She pulled the strap of one of her sandals tight, threaded it through, and stood up. "We studied about some army man getting rid of mosquitoes because they made people sick. So it probably would be okay for you, too. The bites really hurt you, I know."

"I knew you'd give me good advice." Lucy grabbed her sister's hand. "Come on, let's go and get the insects back and surprise Georgie."

The two girls tiptoed out the back door after checking to be sure that their mother was quietly sleeping, book open on her lap. Down the back steps they hurried, along the path to the little mound beside the chicken house. Lucy climbed to the top of the hillock and pulled out the medallion.

Shelley's eyes grew wide when she saw the little dough man begin to glow as Lucy breathed on it. But her eyes grew even wider as she watched what came next.

Lucy made her slow turn, medallion held aloft, crooning softly, "Bug messenger, bring back all the insects but the mosquitoes. Bug messenger, bring back all the insects but the mosquitoes." The air began to fill with the chirr of cicadas and the chirp of the crickets. Bees zoomed from a hidden hive in a tree and butterflies appeared over the basking flowerheads. A dragonfly hovered and darted, disappeared and came back with a friend. An ant skittered over Shelley's foot, followed by two more.

Flies buzzed angrily in the pile of rubbish beside the chicken house and a spider dropped from the corner of the roof and began to spin. As Lucy completed her turn, a shimmering cloud of midges appeared before them.

"There," said Lucy. "The balance of nature is fine now except that I just won't have those horrible mosquitoes around. If I've got the Power of the Wing and Claw and Feather and all that, I should be able to please myself about some things."

Shelley was shocked into stillness by what she had seen. She shook her head slowly. "Lucy, do you realize what you've done?"

Lucy didn't answer. She was busy tucking the medallion away.

"Lucy! Listen to me!"

Lucy looked at her sister, lips folded firmly together.

"You really *do* have a power!" Shelley leaned forward. "You made me better and then did all that with the insects—sending them away and getting them back again. Lucy, there's no telling what you can do!"

"I know. That's the trouble." Lucy squatted down next to her sister. "I know I've got it but I don't know exactly what I'm supposed to do with it.

57

Somehow I've got to find out. Rowan said so."

"Rowan?" Shelley stared at Lucy.

"Yes. Rowan tells me things, and he said that you could help me and Georgie could help, too. It's because of the crown and the flower belly button. You're both part of the Power, too. Will you help me, Shell, please?"

"Lucy, aren't you afraid?" whispered Shelley. "I am."

"All will be well, Shelley," promised Lucy. As before, a wave of relief flowed through Shelley when she heard the words. And this time when Lucy said again, "All will be well," a deeper voice seemed to echo her.

Placing her hand on top of Lucy's, Shelley promised, "I'll help you, Lucy. I'll help you all I can."

FIVE

Contact with Rowan

"It's amazing! Suddenly insects all over the place. And the frogs! The frogs are back, too!" Georgie thrust his spoon deep into the grapefruit half and a golden spurt of juice splashed across the table.

"Georgie, listen to me," ordered Shelley.

"I *hate* eating grapefruit," grumbled Georgie. "It fights back."

Lucy dragged her spoon through the juice making a long golden line on the table.

"Don't make a mess, Lucy. Now listen to me, Georgie. Lucy made the bugs go away and then come back again." Shelley lowered her voice to a whisper. "She really does have the Power of the Rellard."

Georgie looked up, spoon poised, glasses sliding down his nose, and gaped at Shelley. "It was a game. It was just a game we made up!"

"No, it wasn't. Or anyway, it didn't stay a game. Whatever it is, she has some kind of power now."

"Maybe she just thinks so. Maybe it was the poisonous spray that got rid of the insects for a little while and then it wore off and they all came back. Or imagination! You have a lot of imagination, Lucy, you know that. You're always making things up . . . really good things, too, sometimes," Georgie added generously.

"Georgie, it wasn't only the bugs." Shelley mopped up the grapefruit juice and leaned closer to her brother. "She did something else with the Power."

Georgie just looked at her, slowly spooning up another chunk of grapefruit.

"She made my sunburn and fever go away!"

"Mum did that. With the baking soda. You heard her talking about it yesterday, after you got up all better and everything. A real home remedy, she called it."

"Georgie, *I* was the one with the sunburn and *I* was the one lying all sick in my bed. *I* should know!"

"So, what did she do?" Georgie cast a sidelong glance at Lucy, who was calmly munching her way through her third piece of toast.

"She shone the Power on me with that medallion and I felt the sickness lift and go away. I felt it even though I was asleep."

"There you are, it was a dream. You're getting as bad as Lucy, letting your imagination . . ."

"But when I woke up, I was better!"

"So the baking soda worked while you were asleep."

Shelley stood and grabbed Georgie's arm. "Georgie, I saw her bring the insects back."

"You *saw* it!" Georgie whirled on Lucy. "Did she, Lucy? Did you do it when she was there?"

Lucy nodded.

Georgie put down his spoon and shoved his glasses up. For a long moment he just looked at his sister. Then he said, "What are you going to do with this Power?"

Lucy shrugged.

"She doesn't know," Shelley put in.

"Great! That's just great!" Georgie was disgusted. "A little kid like her gets given all this Power! Just gets it handed to her and she doesn't even know what to do with it. Great! Marvelous! What a waste. Why didn't they give it to me? I could think of lots of ways to use it!"

"You're jealous," accused Shelley.

Georgie flushed and looked at the table.

"Look," continued Shelley. "We don't have the Power but she needs us to help her work out what the Power is and how to use it. She *needs* us to help her."

"Well, go on and help her."

"Rowan said that you and Shelley should both help me. He said that you could be my most trusted advisers." Lucy stood and walked to the door. "Let me know when you make up your minds." The screen door slammed behind her. A fly buzzed angrily.

"Rowan? We don't know any Rowan, do we?" Georgie asked.

"No."

Georgie chewed away at his piece of toast. "Well, I suppose we *can* try to help her," he mumbled through the last bite. "Only . . ."

"Only what?"

"Only what if it's all nonsense? I mean, Lucy's been pretty sick and maybe it's made her . . . well, maybe . . ."

"Maybe what?"

"*Funny!* You know. Strange in the head."

Shelley's eyes were serious. "I was there for the insects, Georgie. I saw it. I told you."

"Yeah. That's true." Georgie sat up and straightened his glasses. "Okay—let's go see Lucy and find out more about this Rowan character."

They found Lucy seated in the circle of white stones. The tall trees threw a mosaic of light and shade over her. She was sitting cross-legged, hands resting on her knees, eyes closed. A wreath of clover blossom was draped on her head. She was singing and squeezed her eyes more tightly shut and sang louder when Georgie called out to her.

"Rowan, O Rowan, vay . . . vay . . . Rowan, O Rowan," she sang. Then she stopped and opened her eyes. "It's no good," she said. "I can't find him."

Shelley and Georgie sat down inside the white circle of stones.

"I'll help you, Lucy," said Georgie. "Just tell me what you want to do and I'll help you."

"Thank you." Lucy nodded her head graciously. "Rowan said that you had to choose to help me."

Georgie leaned forward. "Now, who is this Rowan? Tell us from the beginning and don't make it fancy. Just the exact truth."

"Well!" began Lucy, relishing their undivided attention. "It all started after the Bestowal of Power— after you crowned me the Rellard. I was just sitting there and then I heard this man talking in my head."

"Did it hurt or anything?" Georgie was frowning with concentration.

"No. It didn't feel anything. It was just a voice. Like a little radio, in my head."

"Was it this Rowan?"

"I didn't know it was Rowan then because he just talked to me awhile first before he told me what his name was, so I really didn't know. . . ."

"Lucy, don't muddle around. Tell us the straight story." Shelley looked stern.

"He said that I had the Power and that I must learn to use it. Wield it, he called it. And then he said he was named Rowan and he would come and visit me again. Only he hasn't and so I've been trying to call him back, so I can find out more."

"What did he say about me?" Georgie was almost doubled up in a ball, elbows on knees, chin in hands, intent on Lucy.

"Before he stopped talking he said that I needed you and Shell to help me. To be my most Trusted Advisers." Lucy's tone of voice gave the words capital letters. "That's why I needed something from both of you for the Rellard man." She drew out the medallion and dangled it on its dirty shoelace. "It was your piece that went for the crown. Rowan said that you were the head of the Power.

"And you are the energy for the Power, Shelley," continued Lucy. She stroked the flower bead set in the little man's belly. "Because of the flower bead.

And I am the wielder of the Power, here in the right hand." She pointed to the little blue stone.

"Yes, I can see all that, see how it all fits," said Georgie. "But what I can't work out is what it's all for. Why have you been given this Power? What are you supposed to do with it?"

Lucy gazed intently at her brother. "I don't know."

"It seems to me," declared Georgie, "that we should make a concerted effort, a *really* concerted effort to contact this Rowan. But it's a bit hard when he's only a voice."

"I saw him."

"Lucy! Did you! That's important! What did he look like?"

"He has wings, big heavy wings. They're covered in beautiful bluey-green feathers, all shiny. They go all other colors, when he moves the wings."

"I thought you said he was just a voice." Shelley looked skeptical.

"At first he was, but then behind my eyes I saw this man with these beautiful bluey-green wings and it was him. Rowan."

"How do you know it wasn't just your imagination?"

"Because his mouth moved with his words. And anyway, I just knew. It was Rowan."

"Wings! That makes him an angel!" Georgie was incredulous. "Are you sure he has wings, Luce?"

"Yes, I'm sure. Big ones. They stick straight out from his shoulders. But I don't think he's an angel," continued Lucy. "He has horns, here." She pointed to the sides of her head. "They come up in a big curve."

"Are you sure you're not making all this up?" Shelley looked worried. The description of Rowan worried her. An angel? With blue-green wings? And horns?

"No, I'm not. Promise," declared Lucy. "But I can't make him speak to me. I've tried and I've tried. I built this special circle," she pointed to the ring of white stones, "and I've been singing and singing. But he won't speak to me."

"Maybe it's a question of not sending out a strong enough signal," suggested Georgie. "Like when I want more power for my train set, I hook up more batteries."

"Are you going to hook me up to a battery?" Lucy looked worried.

"No, dummy." Georgie settled down to explain what he meant. "You're like a power cell, a little battery, see?" Lucy nodded. "But you aren't sending out a strong enough signal to reach Rowan. Agreed?"

"I suppose so," Lucy agreed.

"Maybe Rowan isn't like a radio," Shelley put in. "Or maybe he isn't even listening or doesn't want to talk to Lucy. Or can't."

"Maybe all your maybes! But let's *try* my theory." Georgie rubbed his glasses on his shirt and hooked them firmly over his ears. "So, to increase the power of your signal, we'll hook in, Shelley and me, like two other batteries, see? And the call—the signal— to Rowan will be that much stronger. Get it?"

Lucy nodded.

"Okay. Now, let's join hands in a circle," continued Georgie, and the three children sat facing in, legs crossed, knees touching, and hands joined. "We'll sing the song together. And *think*, hard, at Rowan. That song you were singing is a calling song for Rowan, isn't it?"

Lucy nodded. "I made it up."

"Maybe the words are wrong." Shelley sniffed. "Maybe Lucy just made up a nothing song."

"Shelley!" Georgie was adamant. "We have to start someplace. And Lucy is the one with the Power, so we should start with her song."

Shelley got a firmer grip on her brother's hand and they began to sing.

"Rowan, O vay . . . vay . . . vay. R . . . vay," they chanted, Shelley's c

67

sustaining Georgie's monotone and providing a contrast for Lucy's softer, huskier tones. "Rowan, O vay, Rowan vay . . . vay . . ." they intoned. "Ishti, vay . . . vay . . . Rowan." The sun climbed through the trees, dropping warm splashes of light. The wreath of clover on Lucy's head wilted and drooped, finally parted, and slid down into her lap. Georgie's face was sweaty. Flies kept buzzing him, and his glasses gradually moved down his nose.

"Oh! Oh! A cramp! My leg—a cramp!" yelped Shelley, and the power circle fell apart.

While Shelley stamped around, working the cramp out of her leg, Georgie and Lucy conferred.

"It's not working. It doesn't feel right, somehow."

Georgie sat thinking, chin in hand. As he watched Shelley's stampings, an intent expression crept up behind his glasses.

"That's it," he announced. "We'll dance it. Singing isn't enough!" He scrambled to his feet, dragging Lucy up with him.

Shelley limped back to the circle. "Have you thought about what you're going to ask Rowan, if he *does* answer you?" she asked.

"Ask him what you're supposed to do with the Power," instructed Georgie.

"But he told her to find out. Remember?" protested Shelley. "We're supposed to help her find out."

"We *are!*" Georgie was adamant. "We're helping her contact Rowan! What he told her, that's not enough instructions for the kind of power she's got. Lucy needs more instructions, lots more." He could tell by the droop in Shelley's shoulders that she wasn't convinced, but her reluctance fired his determination to continue.

"We must dance it, like an Indian powwow dance! Rowan vay . . . vay . . . Rowan, ishti vay . . . vay . . ." he droned, dancing around the circle of white stones, lifting his knees and working his arms like pistons—up, down, up, down. He bobbed his head forward and threw it back, shouting, "Vay! Vay!" Lucy joined him, and at last so did Shelley, dancing around the circle, bending, weaving, throwing their heads back, chanting, louder and louder, "Vay . . . Vay . . . Rowan, ishti vay . . . vay! Vay!"

Their faces grew red with the exertion and their chant became hoarser. Their legs trembled with the effort of lifting and stamping. Finally the three children stopped dancing and stood, panting and dejected. Defeated.

"It's no use." Lucy was close to tears, face pale

beneath the sheen of perspiration. "Rowan won't speak." And she crumpled down to the ground in a heap, cradling her right arm in her lap.

Shelley sat beside her and hugged her close. "Never mind, Lucy. Don't cry."

Georgie squatted down and patted Lucy's shoulder. "Yeah, don't cry about it. We're probably doing it at the wrong time of the day or something." He pulled a handkerchief from his pocket and began to clean his glasses.

The air was still and hot around them as the three children sat huddled together in the white stone circle.

"I think we were wrong to call for Rowan again," said Shelley. "He said Lucy must learn about the Power and we should advise her. I don't think he is there to call, like on a telephone."

"But we don't know what to advise!"

"And I don't know what the Power can do," added Lucy.

"But you're wrong, we *do* know some of the things the Power can do! I think our job, as advisers, is to look at what's happened and work things out. *Not* run to Rowan!"

Georgie perked up. "Make an analysis! That makes sense! An analysis!"

Shelley continued. "Lucy, what have you already

done with the Power? That's what we need to look at."

"I made the insects go away and then I called them back. *You* saw. And I made the mosquitoes *stay* away. Because of the bites."

"That's one thing," said Georgie. "It shows a power over nature. Is that what you mean, Shell?"

"Yes! That's it! And you made me better by taking away the fever and the sunburn, Lucy. That's a power over sickness, isn't it?"

"Of course!" Georgie was getting more and more excited. "Did you bring the Trials notebook, Shelley? You'll have to write all this in it. Draw up a kind of Power Map. Now what else have you done, Lucy?"

"I made the Rellard man."

"How?"

"I used the Orb and baked the little dough man in the Power. So then he was the Rellard man and full of Power, too."

"Like making a nail into a magnet." Georgie nodded.

"What kind of power is that?" asked Shelley. "Not the nail and the magnet but the power in the medallion?"

Georgie considered. "It's the power to make things into talismans, into agents of the Power," he said. "It could be very important. You see, with a talisman, Lucy can spread the Power around, send it out through other things and other people."

"Yes, I see how I could do that," said Lucy. She was sitting up straight now, face pink with excitement. "You *are* helping me, like Rowan said."

"Think hard," urged Shelley. "What else have you done?"

Lucy thought, frowning with the effort. Finally she shook her head. "Nothing else, nothing at all."

Georgie clapped his hands together. "So, we've found three ways Lucy can use the Power. What's the next step?" There was a moment of quiet indecision and then Georgie's eyes lit up. "I know! We'll try an experiment! We'll try an experiment with the Power!"

The three children sat arguing for some time, Shelley reluctant, Georgie gesticulating excitedly and Lucy looking from one to the other. The argument grew more heated. Georgie leaped to his feet and shouted at his sisters.

"It'll be an experiment, all scientific, can't you see?"

Yes, Shelley agreed, she could see about the experiment. But the Power was just that, a *power,* and must be treated with care and consideration. It wasn't to be used for a trivial purpose.

"Trivial!" protested Georgie. "It's not trivial, it will be a really scientific experiment!"

"What experiment?"

"She could fly!"

Both Shelley and Lucy looked taken aback at Georgie's suggestion. Lucy hunched down again and rubbed her arm. Shelley frowned.

Georgie thrust his hands in his pockets. "She wouldn't need to fly very far or very high," he explained. "Just lift herself a little way off the ground, just to see if she can command the Power to do something like that. Just a little experiment."

They decided that Lucy should try to fly up in the air and cross the little circle of white stones. She took the Rellard man out of her shirt and breathed on it, commanding it to make her fly, but the little dough man did not glow and Lucy stayed sitting in the same spot. Georgie thought that she wasn't trying hard enough and urged her to blow harder, but no matter how mightily Lucy puffed and how often she commanded the little man, she did not budge one centimeter.

"We're doing this wrong," insisted Shelley. "Be quiet, you two, and let me think."

Peace descended upon the little group of three in the white circle of stones as Shelley thought, eyes closed, finger twisting a lock of hair. Georgie polished his glasses again and Lucy watched a butterfly dance along under the trees. Finally Shelley spoke.

"Lucy must live the Power," she announced. "She can't experiment with it or order it around. She has to live the Power and it will show itself. And we have to watch and see what the Power does and learn about it. Maybe then when the time comes to use the Power, we will know what to advise."

"That's really what has been happening," Georgie pointed out.

"Yes, but we had to understand it," said Shelley. "It's all in the understanding."

"We didn't need Rowan, after all." Georgie stood and stretched his arms wide. Shelley and Lucy hopped around, kicking the pins and needles out of their legs. Lucy and Georgie moved off toward the cottage, talking. Shelley stared down at the flattened grass in the center of the white circle of stones. She bent and picked up something that was lying there. Running, she caught up with her brother and sister.

"He *was* here!"

Georgie and Lucy stopped, turning blank faces to her.

Shelley thrust out her closed hand and then slowly opened it. There, in her palm, lay a blue-green feather. The sunlight rippled over its surface bringing into play a dance of brighter colors over the deep blue-green below. It was a jewel of a feather.

Lucy laughed and whisked the feather from Shelley's hand. "Yes! Rowan *was* here! And he left us a sign!" She tucked the feather in the wave of hair over her sister's right ear. "Now you wear the Sign of Rowan, Shell!"

They raced to the cottage, the feather a brilliant blue spark in Shelley's golden hair.

SIX

The Emperor Fish Incident

Today was the last real day of the holidays. Tomorrow they would pack and prepare the old cottage for another winter. The children decided to spend this day at the Old Rocky Pool. Shelley had named it that when Lucy was just a baby, and it had become a tradition to visit the place at least once during their time at the Lakes.

The rock pools began at the end of the beach below the cottage. To reach them, you walked down the stone steps to the dock, turned left and churned through the sand until your way was barred by a flat black rock that jutted out of the brambly hillside on your left. Beyond this rock was a tumble of other stones, all mixed up together. They were heaped with all sorts of interesting litter and wrack thrown up by winter storms and packed down by the summer rains. Hidden away from the lake and beach behind this dike of jagged rock and rubble were pools of water.

There were several very small ones, really only chance catchments among the rocks. These appeared and disappeared from year to year. But the biggest was a real pool, a pool that was there every year. Sometimes it was changed a little—showing a little more rock at an edge or muffled by storm debris piled at one side. But generally, the nature of the pool stayed the same. It was big, as big as a small swimming pool. And deep. The bottom was lined with smooth sand between islands of rock and green weed swaying with the currents in the water.

"It's here! It's still here!" Georgie was first there. "It's deeper than last year; don't you think it looks deeper?" He threw down his bundle of gear and knelt beside the pool. Shelley put down her bucket.

"Good Old Rocky Pool!" Shelley said this every year. And every year she spread her arms wide as she said it. It was her salutation to this favorite place.

"That's a silly name, Old Rocky Pool," scorned Lucy. She had felt cranky all morning. "It's a really dumb name."

"You're not supposed to say that things are dumb,

Lucy. It shows a lack in your vocabulary." Georgie began to unpack his gear and assemble a large net on a long telescopic rod.

"Dumb," mouthed Lucy silently at her brother's back, frowning back at Shelley when she caught her sister glaring at her. "That name doesn't show much imagination, that Old Rocky Pool." She wanted to hurt Shelley.

"I don't care what you think, Lucy. It is a good name for this place. And you're not the only one in this family with imagination!" Shelley turned away, back and shoulders stiff with resentment.

"Quick!" Georgie's voice was hoarse with excitement. "I think I see him!" Kneeling beside the pool, face almost touching the surface of the gently moving water, he waved his arm savagely at the girls. "Shadows! Your shadows!" he hissed.

The girls moved around the pool until they were facing the sun, their shadows falling away from the surface of the pool.

"You scared him, letting your shadows fall on the water like that," Georgie accused.

"You probably didn't even see a fish at all," said Lucy sarcastically. "It was probably all in your imagination."

"I'm sure I saw him!" Georgie was indignant. "Come on, you two. Help me watch for him."

Instantly, Lucy felt a flood of remorse. She shouldn't have hurt Shelley, not here, not at Shelley's special place. And Georgie was so excited about his new net and his plans to catch the huge fish that was purported to live in Old Rocky Pool. Lucy heaved a big sigh and lay down full-length on the rocks and began to gaze down into the pool, too. Her sister's reflection danced across the water before her. Lucy rolled halfway over, squinting up at Shelley's silhouette, black against the bright sky.

"Stop towering, Shell, and help us look for him," she invited in a light voice, her coaxing voice. "Please?"

Shelley stood tall and stiff for a moment. Then, with a shrug, she accepted the tacit apology and knelt beside the pool to join in the watching.

Every year Georgie tried to catch the big fish. Every year he insisted that he had seen it, and that it was the same fish, only bigger than last year. Since the girls did not always want to spend hours hanging over the edge of the pool, they were not as sure about the existence of the huge fish as Georgie was. But each of them had, at one time or another, seen a fish in the pool. Today was to be Georgie's big offensive. He was positive his new net would capture the fish and settle the issue once and for all.

"You watch the north end of the pool, Lucy. Especially those rocks there at the corner. He might be hiding in those. Shell, you take the south end and I'll watch the center." Georgie deployed his troops with all the aplomb of an army general. "Don't make any sharp quick movements when you see him. Just give the signal."

The agreed-upon signal was a low whistle. Lucy couldn't manage a whistle. She was to give a kind of wet hiss.

The sun was hot on their backs and played light tricks with the water and the sand and the rocks. Emerald tresses of weed stretched and flowed and aped the movements of a fishy tail. Rocks appeared to be eye and fin and then became rock again.

Lucy was getting bored. She peeped over her shoulder. Georgie was rigidly intent on the water in the pool. His shoulders were braced for action, the new net a tumble of white, close at hand, ready to swoop. Shelley was watching too, not as intently as Georgie, but still scanning her third of the pool in a businesslike way.

Lucy looked back down into the water, wondering what a fish who had lived in this pool for years and years would look like. In her mind's eye she began to build up its image—an Emperor of a Fish, she thought. She traced in the imaginary details, the tall arc of the fins, the round yellow eye, the pink curve of the gills, and finally the mighty fan of a tail, gently propelling the ponderous creature through the subtle currents of the pool.

Blinking, Lucy saw the fish—the huge Emperor Fish! It was real! It was there, moving majestically through the water. She was too astounded to give the signal, but her gasp of astonishment alerted Georgie.

"There he is!" he hissed. "Will you just look at that! Isn't he a beauty?"

Shelley moved cautiously around behind Georgie and came up beside Lucy. "Wow!" she breathed. "He really is a big fish!"

"He's an Emperor Fish," Lucy whispered. "He's lived here in this pool for years and years and years. He's the ruler of this pool. He's an Emperor."

Georgie signaled at them to be quiet and slowly began to lower the net into the water. The cloud of net drifted out from its round gaping rim directly in front of the fish. Georgie held it there for a moment and then began to move it toward the fish, slowly, oh so slowly. The huge, slow fish fanned its tail, stolidly suspended in the clear water.

Both of the girls were excited, urging Georgie on with gasps of encouragement. Crouching, he moved over the rocks at the edge of the pool. Suddenly a flat stone gave beneath his foot, throwing him to his knees. The net jerked from his hands as he fell. It clattered once on the edge of the pool and then flipped into the water, going straight to the bottom. The fish disappeared.

"Oh!" Georgie rocked back and forth, holding his knee. "Oh—oh, damn!" He was close to tears and his glasses were fogging up.

"The net!" Shelley stood, pointing at the bottom of the pool.

Lucy stood too. Shutting her eyes tightly and holding her nose, she fell forward into the water. The force of her plunge was enough to carry her to the bottom of the pool, where she grabbed the net. Shelley and Georgie stood frozen in astonishment as Lucy rose through the water in a cloud of bubbles, net held high.

"Quick! You grab the net!" Shelley leaned forward and made a grab for her sister but missed, fingers slipping along Lucy's arm. Georgie managed to get a grip on the net but Lucy let go, sinking back into the pool in another surge of bubbles.

"Quick! Help her!"

"I've got her! No!"

"Her arm . . . !"

"I'm trying . . . !"

"Oh help . . . !"

It was an age of panic before they were able to

grasp and pull the struggling girl up out of the water and onto the rocks.

"You idiot!" Shelley was trembling with fright and fury. "You . . . ! You . . . !"

"The net," gasped Lucy. "I had to get the net!"

"You can't swim!" Shelley had regained her full voice. "You could have drowned!"

"I forgot." Lucy bent her head to the slow trickle of blood on the knee that had been scraped as she was dragged up over the edge of the pool. "I had to get the net," she repeated, hunching herself into a stubborn knot.

"Thanks, Lucy." Georgie knelt beside his sister, patting her shoulder. "That net cost me a lot. You were really brave to do that!"

Lucy gave him a watery smile and shot a glance up at Shelley, who was still smoldering. "I knew you would save me, Shell," she said.

Shelley fumed her way back to her end of the pool and after a quick noseblow and a mop at the bloody knee with Georgie's towel, Lucy returned to her vigil.

"Hey, I think he's coming out again," breathed Georgie. And surprisingly enough, the huge fish *was* there, sailing sedately through his watery realm.

This time, they were determined to get him. They were caught up in the hunt, crouching low, poised on the rocks, moving their legs and arms with cautious skill—eyes slitted against the sun's glare and the watery sparkle from the pool, voices low, back in the throat, urgent words carrying only to each other, their attention focused on the drifting net that Georgie was lowering through the water; the net that was the extension of their collective will to capture the creature who was drifting so nonchalantly through the waters below. And they did it!

Georgie gave a skillful twist of the wrist and flicked the net down, under and then a mighty haul, up! Up and out of the pool he heaved the great fish, wrenching the thrashing net into the white sunlight, trailing an arc of bright water.

They screamed in delight, all of them, dancing up and down, yelling incoherent words of triumph, arms and legs angular exclamations of joy.

"Got him!" Georgie strained to hold the net. "Got him!" The handle of the net bent with the fish's weight.

"Quick!" Georgie grunted through clenched teeth. "The bucket!"

Shelley ran.

"Fill it up, fill it up with water!" Georgie ordered, braced against the thrashing fury in the net.

"I am! I am!" Shelley yelled back, hastily scooping

up a pail of water and staggering, slopping water as she went, toward the boy.

The fish threw itself in blindly urgent spasms against the net; twisting, turning, wringing the net. Caught, captured, totally enmeshed. Lucy stood frozen, one knee trailing pink water, intent on the fish as it fought against the bright clear death that surrounded it. The strength of the struggling body amazed her, the futile thrusts of the fish fascinated her. Through the net, the eye of the fish gleamed dully. Beneath the white gauze, the bright scales began to fade.

"Here!" Shelley staggered with the weight of the full bucket. She and her brother managed to dump the struggling fish into the pail. It was a tight fit; the fish was so big that it had to bend in an awkward curve. There was little room left for water, most of it splashing over the sides of the bucket.

"Oh you beauty! You beautiful great fish!" crooned Georgie.

"He's huge, he is! Too big for the bucket!" shouted a gleeful Shelley. The two of them began to dance around the bucket, slapping its sides, darting quick fingers into the gaping mouth of the fish, jumping up and shrieking in feigned terror, poking the gills, jangling the handle, laughing, exultant. Georgie squat-

ted down and slapped furiously on the sides of the
bucket with the palms of his hands, then leaped up
to perform a skipping, whooping dance around the
captured fish, savagely triumphant.

Slowly, Lucy walked through their manic caper-
ing until she stood with her toes against the bottom
of the bucket, looking directly down at the fish. He
looked such a poor thing, cramped in that pail, eye
dull, gills feeble. He was stripped of all majesty and
power, all grace and dignity. A captive. A poor,
poor fish.

"Isn't it great, Lucy?" laughed Georgie. "After all
these years, we've finally caught him!"

"He'll taste good. Dad can help us clean him."
Shelley lifted the handle of the bucket. "Help me
carry him, Lucy."

"Taste?" Lucy's face was horror-stricken. "You're
going to eat him?"

"Of course." Georgie was struggling with the in-
tricacies of the rod on his net, which wouldn't col-
lapse. "What else do you catch fish for?"

"But you can't!" Lucy's voice trembled.

"Lucy, don't be silly. Of course we're going to eat
him. *You* eat fish all the time. You *like* fish. Now
come help me carry this bucket."

"But not this fish!"

Georgie turned on her. "Why not this fish? He's

big and fat. Maybe a record catch for the Lakes. They might put my picture in the paper for catching the biggest fish of the year."

"But he's an Emperor Fish. He's not for eating!" Lucy was weeping.

"What?" Shelley was trying to figure this out. "What do you mean, an Emperor Fish? That's no name for a kind of fish. He's a . . ."

"I imagined him!" sobbed Lucy. "In my head, I imagined him and then he was there. He is *my* Emperor Fish."

Shelley looked down at the fish in the bucket.

"You and your imagination!" snorted Georgie. "He's a real fish, I tell you." He threw down the net and went to pick up the other side of the handle. "Come on, Shelley. Let's go."

"Georgie, maybe we should . . ." began Shelley.

"No!" screamed Lucy and she pushed between them, shoving them apart, the bucket overturning, tipping the big fish out onto the rocks. It lay impaled there by the sun, gills gasping, eye gleaming dully, body flopping and twitching.

"Look what you've done!" accused Shelley and bent to grab the fish, which flopped away from her. Georgie grabbed too, and so did Lucy. They danced around the fish, in and out, feet slapping, scrabbling on the rocks, hands grabbing, jerking back, trying to capture the dull, gleaming body that jerked and flopped in ever-weakening spasms.

Lucy knelt beside the fish and spread her arms, sheltering it. "Sh-h-h, sh-h-h-h, sh-h-h," she whispered softly. Slowly she drew in the circle of her arms. The fish, exhausted, lay in one spot, absolutely still.

"Sh-h-h-h, fishy," Lucy crooned. She gently placed her right hand under the head of the fish and closed her left around the base of the tail. Lucy struggled to rise, her right arm trembling with the effort. Finally she stood, the fish clasped in her arms, and walked slowly over to the pool.

"Back to your pool, Emperor Fish," she said, and kneeling, she put the fish into the water. It floated there, briefly, and then quickened, gleamed, and with a flick of its tail, disappeared below the surface.

Lucy watched for a moment. "He's all right, now," she called. "He's swimming." She bent forward. "He's gone in the rocks, now." She turned to face them defiantly, bloody knee trailing pink down her leg.

"He was my Emperor Fish. I imagined him. You can't eat an Emperor Fish!" she declared.

"You're stupid, Lucy." Georgie was almost sobbing in his rage and indignation. "All that work! And the net! Who paid for the net? It was real, I tell you; it was a real fish!" His hands trembled as he fumbled blindly with the handle of his net. "You and your stupid imagination!" he sobbed, and threw the net down.

Shelley, who had not moved from the overturned bucket, walked over to Georgie and put her arm around his heaving shoulders. "Georgie, listen—please, listen to her. This could be important."

"It was important, all right. The biggest fish caught on the Lakes this year and she threw him away!"

"Georgie, she *could* have used the Power to imagine the fish. That could be another way she can use the Power! Think, Georgie!"

Georgie heaved a big breath and turned to look at Shelley.

"It could be, Georgie," Shelley said.

He turned and looked long at Lucy, still standing beside the pool, glaring at them. He sighed. "Okay, Shelley," he said. "Let's hear her story."

They sat in a little circle beside the Old Rocky Pool and listened to Lucy tell how she had become bored with watching and had conjured up the image of the Emperor Fish and how the fish, the exact same fish, had then appeared.

Georgie still entertained a niggling suspicion that the fish had been real, but he reluctantly agreed that they could not eat an imaginary fish, however real he might appear to be. Somewhat mollified, he trailed behind his sisters as they scrambled back over the rocks to the beach. Suddenly he stopped.

"Hey!" he yelled.

They waited for him to catch up. "You know what? We missed out on the really weird thing that Lucy did."

"What weird thing?" Lucy glared at him.

"At the end, when you picked up the fish, he was nearly dead, wasn't he?"

Shelley and Lucy looked at one another.

"But when you put him in the water, he just swam away!" Georgie declared. "Remember?"

"I remember," said Shelley. "He floated a second and then he swam away. I remember!"

"What did you do, Lucy?" Georgie demanded. "What did you do to make the fish come alive so quickly?"

Lucy tucked in her lower lip while she thought. "I just had a picture of him in my mind," she finally said. "I had this picture of him alive and all shiny and strong in my mind, and I looked that picture at him and then he was the same as the picture." She looked from one to the other. "Do you think that was the Power?"

"Yes," said Georgie. Shelley nodded. "That's one

and a half things we've found out about the Power today," continued Georgie as he began to climb the stone steps to the cottage.

"What's the half?" asked Shelley.

"Well, I still only half believe that she imagined that big old fish in the first place," declared Georgie.

Lucy smiled to herself as they climbed.

SEVEN

Rowan Speaks Through the Tree

Shelley drew a picture of the little Rellard man that Lucy wore around her neck and pasted it on the front of the rules of the Trials notebook. It was the Saturday before school was to begin. Later that afternoon, down by the lean-to, she showed the notebook to Lucy and Georgie.

"I've put the dates in, you see," she explained, spreading it open on the arm of the old wicker chair. "And I've described the Ceremony we did after the Trials, and I've started to make a list of the ways Lucy has used the Power."

Lucy didn't look up from her work. She was carefully wrapping the Orb and the Crown in an old pillow slip. A dilapidated wooden box stood open before her.

"What are you doing?" Georgie came to stand over Lucy.

"Putting them away for the winter. Help me make this hole deeper." Using a sharp stick and an old trowel, the two of them dug away at the hole, puffing and grunting and bossing each other until they had a deep pit—as deep as Lucy's right arm could reach. They lined the bottom with some of the white stones from the Lakes and set the little wooden box containing the Crown and the Orb exactly in the center.

Lucy stamped down the earth after Georgie had filled in the hole, and then all of them built a small cairn on the spot, using up the rest of the white painted stones.

"I'll draw a map of where the Orb and the Crown are buried," Georgie said. "Someone could move those stones and then where would we be?"

Hands on hips, he took charge.

"We'll need some points of reference," he explained, "and some units of measure." Lucy sighed and Shelley looked around.

"How about the posts? We could measure a kind of cross from them." Shelley patted one of the posts that supported the vine. "The pile of stones is pretty well in the middle."

"They could burn."

Georgie glared at Lucy. "No one's going to burn

those old posts."

"If they're burned they aren't there anymore, are they?"

"Or someone could take them away." Shelley gripped one of the posts and gave it a good shake. Bits of vine and leaves drifted down on them. "This one's loose. The others probably are, too."

"Okay. We need something more permanent." Georgie looked around. So did Shelley. Lucy got up, dusted off the seat of her jeans and walked around the corner of the shed. Shelley and Georgie looked at each other and followed her.

Down through the vegetable garden, around the rhubarb patch and the strawberry beds they trudged. When they reached the back fence, Georgie balked.

"We're not supposed to go over there, you know we're not."

Lucy calmly climbed through the fence. Shelley followed and so, too, did Georgie, grumbling to himself.

The other side was a tangle of weed, brush, and vines that barred the way to the cellar hole of the old Jacobsen place. Lucy knew the way and the other two were hard put to keep up with her, thrusting aside whippy saplings, feet tangled in weeds. When they finally caught up with their sister, she was standing on top of the tallest upthrust portion of the old granite wall, facing back the way they had come.

"There," she pointed. "The stones are right in a line with this rock and the telephone pole. They can be those point things."

"I hope you didn't drag me all this way for that. Telephone poles can burn, too. Or blow down."

Lucy dropped her arm and looked disappointed. "I just thought this rock would be a good point," she said.

"Here. Let me." Georgie took her place on top of the granite outcrop. "Let me see. Something pretty indestructible, that's what we need." Shading his eyes, Georgie gazed past the distant pile of white stones beside the shed. "Hey!" he exclaimed. "You really get a good view of our place from here, don't you?"

"Hawker Rock." Shelley stopped pulling the burrs from her socks and shaded her eyes, too. "Isn't the Rock in line?" Hawker Rock towered above the town, thrusting out against the river below, forcing it to flow in a wide arc.

"Not really." But, Georgie went on to point out, the little pile of white stones *was* in line with the corner of the house. "We'll consider the house as permanent," said Georgie as he carefully drew in on his map the rock on which he was standing, the corner of the house, and the cairn of white stones. Shelley paced out the number of steps from the corner of the house to the burial spot, keeping in line with Georgie, who signaled with his handkerchief from the granite outcrop.

"Now we need an intersecting line so that whoever is trying to find the spot will know when to stop pacing." Georgie stuck his pencil behind his ear and considered the surroundings.

"But I counted the paces," protested Shelley. "All they have to do is count the same number of paces."

"Some people have long legs." Georgie pointed. "How about using the Big Tree?"

And they did, finding that if they stood at the foot of the tree and sighted on the stone cairn, there was another large stone directly in line. It was being used to support one corner of the shed and half-hidden by the weeds, but it was there and became the fourth reference point on their map.

"Now, here's how it works," explained Georgie and showed the girls how they could find the cairn using the map. "It'll work, even if the cairn is gone."

"You can't see that rock over at the Jacobsen place from here," Lucy pointed out. "Someone will have to stand on it and wave."

"I'll put that in the directions on how to use the

map," and Georgie went into the house for his special mapping pen. He redrew the map with the pen and it was added to the notebook, inside the front cover. He wrote out the directions in a special code that he had made up. The key to the code, he explained, would be hidden inside the stuffed owl in his room.

"Then you can find it and use it if I'm not here. It has to be in a code," he went on. "What if this notebook falls into enemy hands? At least they won't know where the Crown and the Orb are buried. You should write all the rest of the notebook in code, just to be safe!"

"Enemy hands!" scoffed Shelley. "You make it sound like a war!"

"Well, someone might want to get the Power, too, mightn't they?" Georgie looked serious.

They were sitting beside the glowing remains of their bonfire, toasting some ancient marshmallows that Mother had found at the back of the cupboard. Deciding that the wicker chair had had it, they had burnt it and the rag of carpet and the rapidly shredding bamboo mat. Mother had come out to check that they weren't burning the shed, too.

"You've really made a difference here," she remarked, and they looked around in surprise. They *had* made a difference. Now it looked like any other old lean-to beside a shed, with the dry leaves from the vine swept into the fire. It looked bare and clean. The only unusual feature was the neat pile of white stones.

"I suppose you're right, Georgie," said Shelley. She looked worried. "I'll hide the notebook in my treasure box. It has a key."

"It pays to be cautious," pontificated Georgie.

The dying coals of the bonfire winked out, one by one, and the long summer was ended. The three children hugged their knees and shivered in the first cool of the evening.

"Do you think something will happen soon, Lucy?" asked Georgie. "You must have been given the Power for some reason."

"What will it be?" Shelley poked her last marshmallow into the fire. "A natural disaster? An invasion from outer space?"

Lucy hugged her knees tighter and shook her head. "I don't know," she protested. "Don't keep asking me and asking me! I don't know anything!"

Georgie and Shelley gaped at her, astounded at this sudden outburst.

"Well!" Lucy's voice rose petulantly. "That old Rowan, he hasn't told me one single other thing and I haven't been able to make the Power do anything, not since the Emperor Fish, and that was last week, and now I have to go to school!"

There was something in the way that Lucy said *school* that made Shelley wonder if it wasn't the fact that Lucy was going to have to repeat third grade that was worrying her rather than the failure to contact Rowan.

Shelley moved closer to Lucy. "Don't worry," she comforted. "You'll be fine at school. You'll have Miss Reedy for a teacher and she's beautiful. And you'll catch up, you'll see." She put her arm around Lucy.

A wet sniff came from behind Lucy's upturned collar. "It's all right for you," she mumbled.

"Shell and I will have to do some making up on work," put in Georgie. "We got behind, too, while we were at home sick."

"Yes, but you don't have this!" and Lucy thrust out her withered right arm, the twisted fingers of the hand cruelly outlined in the fading light of the fire.

Shelley and Georgie were shocked into silence.

"They'll make fun of me, you know they will," Lucy continued, "or else be sloppy nice. And I can't write with it or draw or anything, not at all! I've tried! I'll have to stay a whole grade behind forever!"

"But Lucy," protested Georgie. "Look how you

won all those Trials. You won them all, fair and square. You're really strong!"

"And you modelled that Rellard man with your left hand. I saw you." Shelley sat up straight. "You'll just have to learn to write with your left hand, that's all."

"You've got the Power, Lucy." Georgie leaned forward, kneeling. "We've seen it."

"I know, I know, but I can't make the Power work all the time. It just comes when it wants to. I can't use it for this," and she held out her right hand. "I tried it today, with the Crown and the Orb, but it didn't work. *That's* why I buried them. They're no good to me now," and Lucy began to cry.

"Lucy, stop this, right now," ordered Shelley. "Now, listen to me."

She read to them from the brown notebook. She read the account of the Trials, all twelve of them. She read the description of the Ceremony of the bestowal of Power and intoned once again the words that had called up the Power. She went on, leaning closer to the light of the fading fire, and read about the sending away of the insects and their recalling, about the sunburn cure and the Emperor Fish. She read about the invisible visit from Rowan and showed them the blue-green feather from his wing, taped to the page. She read about the baking of the Rellard man in the rays from the Orb and how it became a talisman. When she finished, she closed the notebook and leaned forward, peering intently into Lucy's tear-stained face.

"It all happened, Lucy," she said. "It all really happened. You are the Keeper of the Power, which you will be asked to use someday, and we are your helpers and advisers. And you have this." She touched the crumpled, withered hand. "I think there's a balance there, somehow."

Lucy wiped her nose on her sleeve and managed a wan smile.

"Why, that old Rowan might even send you a message tomorrow!" Georgie encouraged, not knowing just how true his forecast was to be. "And don't worry about school. I'll settle anyone who makes fun of you!"

The image of Georgie, a boy in fifth grade involved in a punch-up with a lot of little third-graders, made Lucy giggle, and Shelley joined in too. Even Georgie laughed at himself, after looking a bit put out. Dirty and smoke stained, they doused the fire with water from the pump and went in to supper.

That night there was a storm. Thunder rumbled and roared around Hawker Rock and lightning split the sky. As the wind blew harder, whipping solid sheets of rain against the windows, the main body of the storm marched closer and closer, until at last it raged around their house, thrashing through the trees, lashing shingles from the roof and, in a final paroxysm of enraged lightning, splitting the Big Tree from top to bottom, burying the shed, the lean-to, and the cairn of white stones in its dense foliage as it fell.

Later, as the storm gradually abated, the whole family stood on the back lawn, stunned at the sight of the felled giant, while the rain fell softly on the wreckage.

Dad was up at dawn. "We'll have to get rid of all that," he said, and went next door to get Mr. Carney. Together they rounded up a couple of chainsaws and a pick-up truck and went to work. It was a big job and the saws snarled and shrieked all day, reducing the huge tree to smaller, more manageable proportions. The truck rattled back and forth to the dump, hauling away the twigs and small branches. The Carney boys and their sister, Carrie, along with Shelley and Georgie, carried the sawn logs away, stacking them on the two families' wood heaps.

Lucy refused to help and lay curled up on her bed all day, consenting to come downstairs only when Shelley assured her that the wreckage of the tree was gone.

"It's all cleared up, you're sure?"

"There's nothing left but the stump."

Lucy crept down the stairs and out the back door. It was just getting dark and there seemed to be a lot more sky now, with the Big Tree gone. Down past the shed, past the lean-to, past the pump and around the splintered and singed sandpunt crept Lucy. There before her was the newly cut stump of the great tree. It stood above the ground at the height of her knee.

She climbed slowly onto the stump and knelt there, looking down. Finally she slid face-down on the stump, her cheek resting on the freshly cut wood. She closed her eyes. A lovely smell rose from the wood, tingling in her nostrils. The surface under her cheek felt fresh and cool, clean and new. Her sadness at the death of the Big Tree lifted, and she felt a great calm settling upon her, like a soft blanket spread with a gentle hand.

Into this fresh peace came the voice of Rowan, as clearly as if he were there beneath her in the wood of the stump. Lucy listened intently to the few words that he spoke and then sat up. She scrambled off the stump and stood looking down at it for a moment before she ran up to the house.

Her hair was a mad tangle around her face as she burst into Georgie's room. "You were right! Rowan did send a message! Quick!" And she clattered downstairs to find Shelley.

Georgie dropped his book and ran, too, bumping into Lucy at the kitchen door. Giving Shelley the "come on" signal, they left it to her to explain to their mother why she couldn't, at this exact moment, finish setting the table for dinner, and raced out to the stump of the Big Tree.

"What is it? What's happened?" panted Shelley as she joined them.

"Look," said Georgie. "Rowan's signature."

On the surface of the newly cut stump there was a dark silhouette. It was a bluish color and stood out starkly against the lighter wood around it.

"There! See!" Lucy drew her finger along the edge of the shape. "There are his wings and there and there are the horns. It's Rowan!"

Georgie squinted and tipped his head to one side. "I guess so—but, well . . . one horn seems to be a little crooked."

"He did it with lightning, you know. It's not like a

pencil!" Lucy spread her hand over the dark silhouette. "And that's not all. He spoke to me."

Shelley shivered and hugged herself. Georgie cleared his throat and shoved his glasses up on his nose. "Well?"

"Go on, Lucy," urged Shelley. "What did he say?"

Lucy closed her eyes and leaned on the stump, hands flat, pressing down on the tips of the horns. "He said that we must look to the sky and the waters and that it would be before this tree would branch anew. . . ."

"But," interrupted Georgie, "this tree is dead!"

"Shush," Shelley hissed.

"He said," continued Lucy, eyes squeezed shut, face pale in the gathering dusk, "he said he would speak to both of you."

"Oh, good! How?" demanded Georgie.

Lucy's eyes flew open and she frowned. "That's the part I don't really understand," she said. "He said that Shelley must unravel the riddle of the flower, and you, Georgie, would receive a message by means of the slitted brass."

"I think I'd better write all this down," said Shelley and dashed off to the house for the notebook. But she was intercepted by her mother and sternly ordered to finish setting the table. Georgie and Lucy did not escape their mother's eye either. They were herded up from the stump and sent off to "wash those dirty hands," and from then on, Mum foiled every attempt the three of them made to get together and write down the messages from Rowan.

It wasn't until dinner was over and all the dishes washed, dried, and put away to their mother's satisfaction that they could meet in Georgie's room. Lucy was able to dictate the message to Shelley, who wrote it all down. Georgie tried to sneak down the stairs with his flash camera to take a picture of the silhouette on the stump but was caught by Mum and sent straight to bed.

She told him that they had all had a long day and were overtired and Georgie could take pictures tomorrow after he got home from school.

"I wonder if Rowan realizes how hard it is to deal with the supernatural when you're just a kid and have to do what your mum tells you!" grumbled Georgie as he stamped out of the girls' room after reporting his failure with the camera. "It's not fair!"

Just before she felt herself drifting off to sleep, Lucy remembered the last thing Rowan had said.

"Shelley!" she whispered. "Shelley, listen to me!" she whispered louder. But Shelley was fast asleep.

"I'll tell her tomorrow," thought Lucy, snuggling down. "Beware the lifted hand," she murmured. "That's what he said. Beware the lifted hand." And she slept.

The next morning Lucy completely forgot Rowan's final message in the excitement of getting ready for school. And when Georgie dashed out with his camera to photograph the silhouette of Rowan, despite his mother's warnings that he would be late for school, he found that the blue figure had completely faded away.

EIGHT

A Guardian Is Chosen

"You were right! Miss Reedy *is* beautiful!" Lucy glowed with the success of her first day at school. "She's going to help me catch up and learn to write with this hand and she's *nice!* And so was everyone else!"

"I told you so," laughed Shelley as she ran off to talk to her new friend Suzanne. Shelley had never really had a best friend before, but the new girl seemed to like her and Shelley felt immensely flattered.

"Everyone else wanted to show her around the school—it's her first day—but she asked me to do it. And she's going to be in the marching band, too!" Shelley fairly caroled her news to the family at dinner that night.

"Oh, that's nice. Another musician," said Mum. She was proud of Shelley's musical ability. "It's a talent she got from my side of the family," she would say. Their mother occasionally sat down at the piano and worked her way through a half-remembered étude, humming along with the melody.

Shelley beamed. "She does acrobatics, too! She taught me to turn a cartwheel this afternoon!"

"A cartwheel! What do you want to do that for?" Georgie was astounded.

"It's good exercise. And fun, too. I'm invited over to her house again tomorrow. Can I go, Mum? Please? I'll practice my music lesson in the morning before school, I promise."

"Oh, no, not that!" groaned Dad. Shelley's face fell and then lifted with laughter when she saw Dad wink at Mother. Then they all were laughing, basking in Shelley's happiness.

The new school year was proving successful for another member of the family, too. The next afternoon his mother was frowning over an account book and Lucy was trying to draw the Rowan silhouette with her left hand when Georgie burst into the sunroom.

"Hey! Guess what?"

"Don't throw your books like that!"

"I've been put in a special class!"

"Georgie, those books are going to fall on the floor!"

"It's an advanced class. We get to do all sorts of things!"

"Pick up those books," shouted his mother.

"That's good, Georgie. You're the smartest one in the whole school, I'll bet." Lucy smiled at him over her drawing.

"Mum! Listen!" Georgie pleaded. His face was red and shiny and the bit of tape he had used to mend his glasses was coming unstuck.

"I'll listen when you pick up those books, young man."

Georgie bent and retrieved the fallen books, stacking them on top of each other and shoving them roughly into line.

His mother rubbed her forehead and sighed. "I'm sorry to be so cross. It's these bills." She looked up at her son and smiled. "Now what's this news you're so desperate to relate?"

A special class had been formed for selected children and Georgie was in it. He pulled a crumpled piece of paper out of his pocket. "It tells you all about it. But I have to have your permission before I can go into it on a permanent basis. Mr. Boaz said that."

"Mr. Boaz?" His mother looked up from the letter. "Who is he? A new teacher?"

"He's a genius, Mum. Really he is. He's a real scientist and he's planned all sorts of real scientific work for us to do." Georgie tipped forward on his chair, reaching across the table with outspread arms. "It tells you there in the letter some of the projects we'll do. And you and Dad just have to sign at the bottom. And it doesn't cost anything extra," he added, catching her glance at the account book. "Please? Can I be in the class?"

"I'll have to talk it over with your father." Mum folded the letter with careful fingers. "But I don't think there will be any difficulty." She smiled.

"Great!" Georgie's face lit up and he jumped to his feet.

"Georgie!" Mum warned, but the chair tipped over with a crash and the books slithered in a series of thumps to the floor as Georgie scrambled to rescue them. Mum folded her lips in exasperation as Lucy ran to help rescue the books. She followed Georgie to his room.

"That's good about the special class," Lucy said.

"Yes. It's an invaluable opportunity to do some real scientific experiments and things. That's what Mr. Boaz said. An *inval*uable opportunity." Georgie cleared a space on his desk for the books.

"Miss Reedy is nice, too. She's got a smiley kind of face. What does Mr. Boaz look like?"

"He's serious and he frowns a lot."

"Frowns? Doesn't that scare you?"

"He doesn't frown angry." Georgie stood, head on one side, considering. "It's more a thinking frown, like he's going over all these problems in his head all the time and solving them."

"Doesn't he ever look happy?" Lucy perched on the end of Georgie's bed. "I couldn't stand it if Miss Reedy frowned at me all the time."

"He doesn't believe in emotions." Georgie began to sift through the pile of debris at the bottom of his closet. "Have you seen my compass, Lucy?"

"No. Why doesn't he believe in emotions? What's emotions?"

"Lucy, I'm busy. Love and hate and fear and happiness and things like that. Rats! Where's that compass?"

"Look in that drawer." Lucy pointed to the dresser. "How can you not believe in happiness?"

"He said emotions cloud the mind. We have to learn to be objective. Hey, Luce, you were right. Here it is!" and Georgie lifted the compass out of the drawer, its lanyard tangled in the tines of a tuning fork.

"Georgie, can you help me draw what we saw on the stump?"

"What?" Georgie stuffed the compass into his pocket and began to pull on his boots.

"The Rowan thing. On the stump."

"Oh, yeah, the silhouette. Sorry, Lucy. Can't. Going on a short hike up to the Rock. I have to take some notes on plants for class tomorrow, for Mr. Boaz's class."

"Have you thought about the message?"

"Where's my little black notebook? I had that notebook here just a couple of days ago." Georgie began to paw through the pile of papers, folders, and files in a basket on his desk marked "Pending."

"Try the top righthand drawer of your desk." Lucy bounced on the end of the bed. "The message from Rowan about the slitted brass."

"Hey, it's here! You're a good finder, Luce!" Georgie grabbed a pencil. "The slitted brass? Yes, I thought about it but I can't figure it out. Have to go now. Come on. I don't want you to stay in here when I'm not here. You might mess things up."

Lucy gave one last bounce on the end of the bed before allowing her brother to herd her out the door.

"Tonight after dinner? The *silliet* thing?" she called down the stairs after Georgie. "Will you help me?"

"Yeah, sure." And Georgie banged out the front door leaving Lucy to kick at the banister.

"I'll ask Shell to help me when she gets home." Lucy sighed. She trudged downstairs to the sunroom, where her mother was still glaring at the account books.

But when Shelley arrived she wasn't interested in the silhouette or the riddle of the flower. And that was the pattern for the next few weeks. Shelley spent every available minute after school with Suzanne.

"Her middle name is Quincey, so she's called Susie Q," Shelley informed the family at dinner one evening. Georgie made a gagging noise but was quelled by Mother's glare. The part of Shelley's life that was not occupied with Suzanne was taken up with piano and clarinet practice, band practice and as much time as the rest of the family would allow her to have in the bathroom. Boys flocked around Susie Q, and Shelley was trying to do things with her hair. She spent hours combing it, washing it, rolling it up, and taking it down, imitating the toss of the head that showed off her friend's sweep of blond hair to advantage.

Georgie spent every waking moment thinking about or being with Mr. Boaz. He went to school early to work with the teacher, stayed after school for more work, and went on scientific explorations of the area with his idol on weekends.

The little town of Springdale was situated in a fertile valley with a river winding through on one side. Over the centuries the river had cut away at the base of the hills, carving the high cliffs that towered over the north side of the town. That area was all a state park now.

The weather stayed warm and Mr. Boaz took his little troop of scientists on explorations just about every day. Georgie was getting thinner from all the tramping and climbing, and he always came back laden with specimens. Every evening was taken up with his notes.

"Mr. Boaz says you must transcribe your notes as soon as possible, otherwise valuable information will be lost," he would say importantly, and disappear into his room, the "Do Not Disturb" sign draped over the doorknob.

Mum and Dad were spending more and more evenings "going over the books," so after dinner Lucy was left to herself. She did her homework for Miss Reedy, working hard to force her awkward left hand to trace out the letters and numbers. She gave up trying to interest Georgie and Shelley in the Rowan silhouette and folded the drawing she had made away in a drawer. She puzzled over the messages but couldn't think what they meant.

She also tried out little experiments with the Power. She used it to find lost things, but as she had always been what her father called "a good finder," no one noticed. She wasn't sure herself if the Power was helping her locate the lost things or if it was just a matter of luck, so she didn't mention it and Shelley didn't put that use of the Power in the notebook.

Lucy also used the Power on Miss Reedy and the children in her class, trying to get to know them. She had always been shy, and now her withered hand and arm made her shyer still. She always wore the Rellard man medallion under her blouse or sweater, and in class she would clasp it in her hand and concentrate on whoever she was trying to "read." Mostly she found out how the person felt at the time, picking up little waves of happiness or boredom or frustration. But sometimes the people-reading gave her whole words instead of just feelings. And with one child in the class she could hear what was going on in his mind as if it were a radio broadcast.

This child was Joey, so small that his feet swung clear of the floor under the desk. He had big ears and pale, freckled skin.

"Help me can't do that—why is she making me

do that oh wrong all wrong bad bad broken pencil help he looking she looking bad can't can't can't . . ." Joey's thoughts were borne in on a wave of trembling fear. Lucy was mildly astonished at the clutter of Joey's thoughts, but she was not really surprised to find that he was scared of everyone and everything. He *looked* scared, from the wispy-haired top of his head down to his scuffed tennis shoes.

She tried to use the Power in reverse, broadcasting clear helpful thoughts to him, gripping the little dough man hard in her hand, but although Joey was a most efficient sender, he was a hopeless receiver. No matter how hard she sent messages to him, his mind clattered around and around on its endless shuttle of "help" and "can't."

So Lucy gave up sending thoughts and sat with Joey at lunchtime, getting him to talk. It was slow work. She had to tell him not to be afraid, just straight out, "Don't be scared, Joey," and then keep on saying it, for every little thing.

Like, "Don't be afraid to sharpen your pencil, Joey. Miss Reedy said you can do it if you don't talk on the way to the pencil sharpener. You don't have to have special permission." Or: "Put up your hand and *ask* when you have to go to the toilet! Miss Reedy's nice. She'll believe you."

Joey was still pretty scared but at least he was

sharpening his pencil and asking permission to go to the toilet when he was desperate. And sometimes he smiled at Lucy.

Lucy missed the time with Shelley and Georgie, but her mother was always there when she came home from school. She talked to Lucy about Miss Reedy and school and Joey.

One Thursday in autumn, Joey came home from school with Lucy to play. It was a warm day and they made roads down in the sandpunt even though most of the sand was gone and it wasn't the same without the Big Tree sheltering them. But poor Joey didn't really know how to play and went home early, trailing a little cloud of "can't-oh-help-me-can't-oh-help" behind. Lucy sighed and went up to the house to talk to Mother.

Later, after it was all over, Shelley and Georgie tried to remember how the bad time had started.

"I want to write it down, properly, in the notebook," Shelley said, "but I don't know where to start."

"It was simultaneous," Georgie stated. "Boom! All together! All at once! Just like that!" He slapped his hands together.

"Not really—not quite," Shelley insisted. "Anyway, I can't write it down all at once, it will be muddled. I'll have to start with one thing and then go back for the next."

" 'Spose so."

"You're not being very helpful."

"No. It was some of our fault, you know, the part about Lucy. We didn't pay enough attention to her."

"Georgie, stop that. We couldn't help it. We were influenced."

"I still think that if we'd just paid a little bit more attention, we could have seen it all coming, could have helped her more at the beginning. It wouldn't have been so tough in the end, then."

"Maybe we could have but we didn't. Now tell me what you think was the beginning of the bad time."

"Dad getting sick," Georgie stated firmly. "Mum crying. That was the real beginning."

The bad time started—really began—just when Lucy arrived back at the house that afternoon that Joey went home early. Her mother was in the kitchen, white-faced, grim, slamming cupboard doors, lunging from refrigerator to sink to stove, crashing lids onto pots and pans, stamping so hard on the foot lever of the garbage bin that the thrust of the opening lid threw the bin over, sliding it out from under her toe. Potato peelings and carrot tops splattered across the floor, and a sprinkle of coffee grounds dribbled past the half-open lid of the toppled bin. Mum burst into tears and Dad came rushing.

"What the . . . ?" he shouted in an angry voice, and then he put his arms around Mum and patted her shoulder, one hand rubbing up and down on her arm.

"What's the matter?" Lucy stood just inside the back door. "What's happened?" Her stomach felt cold. Her mother! Crying! And Dad home early? "What is it? What . . ."

"Lucy, dear, just go on up to your room for a minute, okay? Just go and talk to Shelley for a little while. It's okay, everything's fine." Dad kept on patting Mum's back as he spoke.

Lucy stepped carefully around the garbage on the floor. She stopped and stooped to pick up the bin.

"No, just leave that," her dad said. "Just go on up to your room, that's a good girl," all the while patting. Mum was still crying.

Lucy dashed up to the bedroom. No Shelley!

"Help! Shelley!" she whimpered, and ran on down the hall to the bathroom, where she banged on the closed door.

"Shelley! Help! Shelley, are you there?"

The sound of running water stopped.

"Yes. Go away." Shelley sounded as though her head was in a towel.

"Shelley, open the door. Something terrible has happened. Please!"

Shelley's answer was to turn on the water again. Lucy leaned against the door and closed her eyes.

"*Please,* Shelley," she begged. "Open the door. I *need* you."

"I'm almost finished. Go find Georgie. I'm putting conditioner on my hair."

"Shelley, Mum's crying in the kitchen!"

The door to the bathroom snapped open without any warning. Lucy almost fell into Shelley's arms.

"What did you say?"

"Mum! She's crying! Down in the kitchen."

"She must be really upset," said Shelley thoughtfully.

"Shelley, she's *crying!*"

"It's the job. Go on and tell Georgie while I finish my hair." The door shut firmly.

"What job?" Lucy asked the door, then turned to run back to Georgie's room. For once the door was open. Georgie was on the floor, sorting out what looked like bits of bone in the bottom of a box.

"Mum's crying and Shelley is doing her hair and what does she mean about a job?"

Georgie carefully transferred a bit of bone from the box to an envelope. He was using a pair of tweezers.

"Georgie, answer me!"

"Mum is going to work, because of business being bad and the mortgage," Georgie said. He made a note on the envelope.

"What mortgage? What is it—a mortgage?" Lucy's voice cracked.

Georgie put down his tweezers and pointed out that Dad's photographic studio was not doing so well. He explained that because of this there wasn't enough money to pay the bank for the money used to buy the house and the building the studio was in. He explained that their mother was going to work in the studio with Dad.

"You've seen her working on the account books," Georgie said. "Didn't you wonder what she was doing?"

"She's always worked on those old account books! She's done them here at home!"

"Yes, but she hasn't always frowned while she did them. And there's been more expenses this year." Georgie glanced at Lucy's limp hand. "Us being sick and everything."

"It's my fault? Is it my fault she's crying?" Tears tightened Lucy's throat.

"No, Lucy, don't be silly." Shelley came in the door, rubbing her head vigorously. "It's no one's fault. Business has been bad. Dad said so. Elsie at the studio is leaving and Mum's going to do her job. To save the salary, you see? Just until business picks up a bit."

"But why is she crying like that?" Shelley and Georgie looked at each other.

"You're not telling me everything, are you? It's not just the job. What else? What is it?" demanded Lucy.

"It's Dad. He's sick." Shelley lowered her voice even further. "That's the other reason Mum's going to work with him, to help him."

"But how do you know? Why didn't they tell me?"

"They wanted to get all the arrangements settled first. They didn't want to scare you. You're the youngest. It's heart trouble. Dad's got heart trouble." Georgie looked solemn.

Lucy sat down on the end of Georgie's bed. Heart trouble! She pressed her hand to her chest and felt her own heart beating there. Heart trouble! What did it mean? Would Dad's heart stop?

"Will he die?" she whispered.

"What's this? Why so solemn? Come on—up, all of you, and downstairs. We're going to have a family meeting!" Dad was standing in the door, a bit pale, but still Dad, with his crinkly smile, joking them up onto their feet, down the stairs, where they all sat around the dining-room table and tried not to look at their mother's tear-streaked face.

Dad explained it all to them in a quiet steady voice. A new photographer had come to town and taken a lot of the business away from him. "He's working for a big company and can undercut my prices. But he can't do that forever. And quality counts!" Dad waggled a finger at them. The studio couldn't afford a paid assistant like Elsie, now. But at the same time the doctor had said Dad must not work so hard on account of his heart. "Bit weak in the old pump." Dad laughed, looking around the circle of serious faces. So the solution was obvious. Mum was going to work in the studio. And that was that.

"You're all old enough to help out and it won't be for long," Dad promised. "First we have to work out what to do about you three coming home from school when your mother's not here."

Shelley had her after-school lessons in music. "And I can go to Suzanne's house the other days. Her mother said so." Shelley's hair hung damp and clean, swinging smoothly when she turned her head.

"Mr. Boaz wants me to stay and help him," said

Georgie. "He's always asking me to be his assistant. It'll be fine with him."

But Lucy! What to do with Lucy?

"I'll ask Miss Reedy if you can stay an extra half an hour at school, and then Carrie can pick you up on her way home and stay with you until I get here." Her mother's voice trembled a bit.

"Carrie!" The three children considered the Carney clan more as an enemy camp than as neighbors. Carrie, years older, was an unknown quantity. She never involved herself in the noisy melées with her brothers and the other children in the neighborhood.

"She needs the little bit of money I'll pay her and she volunteered. She likes you, Lucy." Mum stood and went to the kitchen.

"Well, that's it then!" Dad went into the living room to read the paper, Georgie returned to his box of bones and Shelley began to set the table for dinner.

Lucy hung on the edge of the kitchen door, swinging away when Shelley passed through laden with plates and silverware, coming around again to watch her mother, busy at the stove.

"Mum?"

"M-m-m-m-m?"

"How do you know she likes me?"

"Who, dear?"

"Carrie. How do you know?"

"She said so. Here, put this on the table for me."

Lucy returned to the kitchen door. "What did she say?"

"Who?"

"Carrie. What did she say when she said she liked me?"

"Now let me see." Her mother stood, potato-masher poised, thinking. "Oh, yes. It was the tree. She said she saw you in the Big Tree. She didn't really say that she liked you, she said she'd like to look after you. But it's the same thing."

Lucy shivered and swung on the door. She wasn't sure it was the same thing at all.

NINE

Danger for Lucy

It began to rain in the night, a steady ruthless rain that stripped the leaves from the trees and piled them in soggy heaps in the gutters. It was a chilling rain, falling from a sky drained of any light, dulling the ordinary breakfast sounds of spoon on dish and dimming the usually bright kitchen to a half-light.

Shelley and Georgic left early after thumping and bumping into their boots and raincoats in the front hall. Dad was already away, trying to get ahead on the darkroom work. Mum and Lucy left the house last.

"The key is under the mat, Lucy. I told Carrie, but you need to know, too. Don't lose that note for Miss Reedy." Mum bent down to kiss Lucy on the nose. "I'll see you tonight!" Her red umbrella bobbed down the hill.

Halfway up the next block, Lucy turned and looked back at her home. Its windows were dark. She imagined herself running back to the lonely house, snatching up the key, and letting herself in. She could stay home all day and keep the house company! A gust of wind blew rain up under the broad brim of her rain hat, blotting out her view of the house. No, she couldn't keep the house company, she had to go to school.

Miss Reedy! Lucy's heart lifted as she turned to trudge on toward the school. She would talk to Miss Reedy about Mum's job after she had showed her the note. Maybe Miss Reedy would put her arm around her!

And Miss Reedy did exactly that, resting her soft arm on Lucy's shoulder as she told her how nice it would be to have that extra half an hour together. A breath of perfume enveloped Lucy as she stood close to Miss Reedy, so close she could see the fine down on her teacher's cheek. Lucy was happy.

After school, the extra time zipped by. Lucy was engrossed in watering the plants that lined the window sills of the classroom and had to rush to finish so as not to keep Carrie waiting.

Carrie turned out to be better than Lucy had expected. They didn't have a lot to say to each other, but the walk home through the chilly rain was accomplished in a companionable silence. Furthermore, Carrie took her duties very seriously, going through the whole house after letting them in with the key from under the mat, looking in all the rooms, checking doors and windows.

"Why are you doing that?" Lucy carefully poured two glasses of milk.

"Doing what?" Carrie came back into the kitchen and began unpacking her books onto the kitchen table. She was going to study until Lucy's mother arrived home.

"All that checking on the windows and things."

"Just being sure." Carrie sat down and opened a book. She got out a blank pad of paper and clicked her ballpoint pen out to the ready.

"Who do you think might be here?" Lucy persisted.

Carrie looked at her thoughtfully. "I don't know." She frowned. "I just feel that I should look." She smiled her slow smile. "Have to look after you, you know."

Lucy felt safe with Carrie, safe and a little lonely. She missed Georgie and Shelley. She fretted because the Power seemed to have been forgotten by them.

She had had no further communication with Rowan even though she sang her calling song a couple of times. She felt that the whole experience last year— Rowan, the Power of the Rellard, the signs—all of it was slipping away like a half-remembered dream.

And she was worried. She had the nagging feeling that something was not right, not really as it should be. It was a relief to find that Carrie was so cautious and would watch over her carefully.

"When did you see me in the Big Tree?" she asked. The kitchen light was bright against the gray rain outside. It was raining harder.

Carrie looked up from her work. "The Big Tree?"

"You know, the one that got lightninged."

"*Struck* by lightning." Carrie laughed.

"When?" asked Lucy.

There was a short silence filled with the sound of the rain. Then Carrie spoke. "Just one day, I saw you." She bent her head to her book again but Lucy noticed that her eyes weren't moving across the lines of text.

"What day?" It was important for Lucy to know what Carrie had seen. "What was I doing?"

Carrie kept her head down. "Last summer, one day last summer, I saw you." Carrie's voice stopped and she turned the page, even though Lucy was positive she hadn't read it. "You had a red scarf or something," Carrie continued. Suddenly she looked up, staring full into Lucy's eyes.

"You climbed up that tree fast!" Her face was very serious.

Lucy nodded.

"And then when you got to the top," Carrie leaned forward, her voice deeper and more intense, "something happened to the tree. I saw it!"

Lucy could only stare back at the older girl.

"Did you see it?" Carrie was leaning far forward now, her hand out on the table, reaching toward Lucy. "Did you? Did you see it, too?"

Lucy nodded.

Carrie heaved a huge sigh of relief and sat back in her chair. She smiled at Lucy, a conspiratorial smile. "So we're both crazy!" She laughed. Then her face grew sober.

"That's why I have to look after you. You're special—or something."

Now it was Lucy's turn to sigh with relief.

And that was all Carrie ever said on the subject. With Lucy's mother she talked about how the money she received for looking after Lucy was a help, but Lucy knew that Carrie would have taken over the afternoon watches without the money.

"You all right at school?" she asked one day as they walked along hunched against the wind.

"Sure. I'm fine. Miss Reedy's a good teacher."

"She doesn't pick on you or anything?"

Lucy was shocked. Miss Reedy? Pick on *her*? Lucy?

"Why?"

Carrie frowned. "I don't know."

Lucy tried out the Power then. She had given up using it much at school because she really didn't need it. Joey talked to her now, and so did the other children. She had lots of friends. There was Jeremy, who helped her do the guppy's bowl, and Sheryl, who told her secrets, and all the others. She didn't need to look into their minds with the Power.

But today, walking through the cold wind with Carrie, she suddenly felt that it was important to understand what the older girl was trying to say. Lucy reached under her coat and clasped the little Rellard man and concentrated. The lumpy little man felt warm through her mitten.

She was stopped in her tracks by the sudden wave of apprehension that flooded into her mind. Carrie was not just worried, she was afraid! Very, *very* afraid. And she was afraid *for her,* Lucy. Running, she caught Carrie's hand in her own.

"What is it? Why did you ask me if I was all right?"

Carrie frowned down at her.

"I don't know," she insisted. "I don't know! Just you be careful, see?"

That afternoon she was meticulous in her check of the house, going over all the windows and doors, even climbing down to the cellar, where the heating system hummed and clicked away to itself. Lucy followed along behind, and even though there was no one there, neither felt reassured as they sat down at the kitchen table—Carrie to study and Lucy to color in her diagram of the ear. Lucy knew that Carrie was afraid that something bad was going to happen to her, Lucy. To tell the truth, Lucy was getting a bit worried herself. Something wasn't right.

But who could she talk to? Her mother was so worried about her father—it showed in her eyes and around her mouth. And what could Lucy say? It was just a feeling, an uneasy worried feeling that she shared with Carrie.

She would have gone to Shelley and Georgie but since school had started, they had moved off into separate worlds. Shelley had no time for Lucy now. She had Suzanne and her music and Suzanne and the marching band and Suzanne.

Georgie was the objective scientist.

"Objectionable scientist, you mean!" Shelley

snapped when he sternly scolded her for letting her emotions control her intellect. "You're awful with all your facts, facts, facts!" and she stormed up to her room. Lucy was sure Georgie would have no time for her fearful feelings.

The weather deteriorated quickly that year. Once the autumn rains began they never really stopped. It just kept on raining, a cold, chill, dismal rain that gradually merged into sleet and snow as the temperature dropped. In no time there was quite a bit of snow on the ground and people were talking about it being the coldest winter on record. The sun seemed to have disappeared. The sky was always gray and dark, flinging down snow or sleet or cold rain. Trees bowed and broke under the weight of the ice and snow. The inside of their house developed cold areas that just grew chillier, even with the central heating on.

"We have to save money on fuel this year," Mother announced and turned the thermostat down. "Put on more clothes," she ordered. They did, but the house still felt cold and dismal. Only when Dad brought in some of the wood from the Big Tree to burn in the fireplace did the air in the house seem to lighten and grow warmer. But the wood was still too green and wet to burn well. It hissed and spat and sent out smoky signals.

"Next year it will be better for burning," promised Dad.

Georgie had set up a little weather station outside the kitchen window and was keeping a log of the temperature as well as measuring the precipitation. He was making a graph that compared this year's temperatures with last year's as well as the average for the last ten years. He had it stuck up on the wall beside the refrigerator.

"Hey!" Dad stopped in front of the chart one morning. "Are you sure this is right?" He traced with his finger the lowest line on the chart, the cold blue line for this year's temperature. It was a long way below the other two lines and was getting lower all the time.

Georgie bristled. "I've checked it every day. And I'm using two thermometers. It's absolutely correct to within a hundredth of a degree!"

"Absolutely?" Dad teased but Georgie didn't think it was funny. "Sure seems strange. Getting so cold like that." Dad grew sober again.

"These things come in cycles, Mr. Boaz says," Georgie explained. "Over the long range it will even out."

"Over the short range it's cold!" Dad laughed. "Bit depressing, too."

Lucy waited until Dad left the room. "Georgie,

maybe that's what Rowan meant the Power was for. The cold, I mean."

"Don't be silly!" Georgie's eyes always seemed to hide behind his glasses now. "That was just a game, Lucy, you know it was."

"But what about the insects and the fish and . . ." Lucy was desperate. Surely it hadn't been just a game! Surely she had heard Rowan speak! Surely she had the Power!

"All of it can be explained scientifically, you know it can!" Georgie shrugged. "Besides, *I* never saw anything magic."

"The fish?"

"The water revived him."

"The *silliet*?"

"Sil*hou*ette. You can make anything from a shape like that. It was just your imagination, Lucy. Mr. Boaz says that too much imagination weakens the mind!"

Lucy was too hurt to answer. A weak mind! Is that what was wrong with her? She held the little Rellard medallion firmly but it did not warm in her hand. She could not pick up Georgie's thoughts at all.

Shelley, when she was asked for it, couldn't produce the notebook in which she had written of the Rellard summer, as Lucy called it in her mind.

"I don't *know* where it is, Lucy. Please leave me alone. I'm busy."

When Lucy brought up the subject of the Rellard and Rowan and the signs, Shelley seemed embarrassed and then angry.

"It was just a game, Lucy, just a holiday game!"

"But the insects? You saw the bugs come back!" Lucy begged. But Shelley wouldn't answer and turned away from Lucy, telling her to go away, to stop being a baby.

Lucy felt very alone then. Carrie was the only one who showed the least concern for her and it was an unfocused concern that just added to Lucy's feeling of isolation and uneasiness. The creeping, insidious cold seemed to have permeated her life, freezing the lines of communication with her family. She was alone and the Power that only she now believed in seemed to have deserted her. She felt her own belief shrinking, eroding, being slowly dissipated by the cold unbelief of her brother and sister.

"Oh, Rowan," she breathed into her pillow, her hand clasping the little medallion under the blankets. The night was very dark, snow whispering beyond the walls, piling itself on the window sill. "What am I to do?" she asked.

There was no answer.

The next day Lucy left the medallion rolled up in

a sock in her top drawer. When she arrived at school, Miss Reedy was not there. Seated in her place was an older woman with a smooth plain face.

"My name is Mrs. Gibbs," she wrote on the board in large, flowing script. She carefully placed the chalk in the tray below the board and dusted her fingers on a white handkerchief. She turned to face the silent class.

"Miss Reedy has been called away," she said. "It may be some time before she returns. Until she does, I will be your teacher."

She stepped forward and moved to the head of the first row of desks. Her voice was very deep and stern and she towered above Jeremy, whose desk was first in the row.

"Stand and give your name—your full name—and your age. Begin here," she ordered, and pointed to Jeremy.

Jeremy caught his foot trying to get out of his desk and knocked everything to the floor. His voice came out a squeak and then gave up altogether. It was an inauspicious beginning and things got worse as each child gave his or her name and age to the unsmiling Mrs. Gibbs. She moved down the aisle between the desks, standing close to each child. Some tipped their heads far back, trying to speak to her face. Others, like Joey, looked at the floor and were made to repeat and repeat their names until Mrs. Gibbs was satisfied. Some stoically shouted at the woman's midriff, not willing to look at her curiously blank face.

She's looking for someone, thought Lucy, hugging her right arm, dreading her turn to stand before this tall woman. Lucy shivered. She didn't like this woman, didn't like her at all. Why did Miss Reedy have to go away and leave her with this woman? Her heart beat rapidly and she swallowed hard, trying to loosen her throat.

Mrs. Gibbs was two desks away now. Now only one, as Sheryl stood and gave her name in a clear voice. The woman's direct gaze shifted to Lucy, and as their eyes locked, Lucy's breath caught in her throat and her toes curled in her shoes. She tried to stand up but couldn't move, caught in the dark gaze of the woman who now stood directly above her.

"Ah," the woman breathed softly. "Ah!"

Lucy knew that the woman had been looking for someone and that the search was ended. She had been looking for Lucy.

TEN

The Slitted Brass Solved

On the last day of the school term, Georgie arrived home before Carrie and Lucy. He had to scrape the snow off the doormat before he could lift it to find the key. Muttering as he struggled to turn the key in the cold lock, he then faced around and backed into the front hallway. He had the notion that if he moved backwards into the warmer house from the cold outdoors, his glasses wouldn't get fogged. So, because he was facing the wrong way, he completely missed the brown-wrapped magazine that had rolled against the wall away from the pile of mail that the postman had pushed through the metal flap in the front door.

Georgie scooped up the rest of the mail and dumped it on the table before going up to his room.

As he climbed the stairs he rubbed away absently on his fogged glasses, thinking about his latest project, which was sure to impress Mr. Boaz.

Dad noticed the brown roll against the wall and brought it up to Georgie's room.

"Some mail for you." He smiled around the door. He tossed the magazine to Georgie. "How's it going?"

Georgie really didn't want to waste time talking to his father. He was sitting at his desk underlining headings in red ink and bracketing procedures in blue. He picked up his green pen to start putting green boxes around the expected results and grunted a noncommittal "Okay, thanks," and tossed the roll on top of the heap in his in-tray.

Downstairs, Lucy heard her father tell Mum that he wasn't sure if he approved of the effect that Mr. Boaz was having on Georgie. "He thinks he's too smart," grumbled Dad and crackled the newspaper. "He'll have to learn to keep a civil tongue in his head!"

Meanwhile, Georgie worked on in the bright oasis of light thrown on his desk by the lamp. He whistled quietly through his teeth as he ruled the neat lines on the page. The room was quiet and chilly. Snow was falling gently against the window, gradually drawing a white shutter up from the sill.

Bit by bit Georgie became aware of something softly pushing against the circle of his concentration. He looked at the door. Closed. No one there. He looked all around the room. Empty. The owl gazed at him from the top of the bookcase. No one. Nothing. It must be the snow, brushing the window. He got up and drew the blind down.

There was still something niggling away on the edges of his thoughts.

I'm cold, Georgie thought and put on another sweater. But when he sat down at his desk he could not work. Something, someone was trying to get his attention.

"Ridiculous!" he thought and resolutely picked up his green pen.

That was when the brown-wrapped magazine rolled off the piled-up contents of the in-tray, bumped down onto the desk, and kept rolling until it came to rest against the tip of his pen.

Georgie stared at the magazine for a moment and then picked it up, turning it around and around. The label had his name and address on it, clearly typed. The postmark was blurred and had run into the brown paper. There was no return address or company name anywhere on the wrapper.

Georgie put the wrapped magazine down on his desk, away from the neatly inked and ruled page before him and picked up his pen once again. The magazine rolled forward and stopped in the middle of the page.

The back of Georgie's neck felt cold. He stared at the magazine, then pushed it off the paper with his pen. It rolled back again and sat, gently rocking, right in the middle of his project page. Georgie's hands shook slightly as he picked up the package and began to undo the wrapper.

"A comic!" he gasped. "Just a rotten old comic book!" He was indignant. Who could be sending him comic books? He hadn't read any comics since going into Mr. Boaz's special class. Mr. Boaz said that comics were juvenile and that a boy with his caliber of mind shouldn't waste his time on such rubbish. Georgie had stacked his huge collection of comics in the back of the cupboard. He couldn't bring himself to throw them away, but at least they were out of sight. He read only books about real things now, books with facts and diagrams and photographs. Occasionally he checked the back of his cupboard to be sure the comics were still there.

But what a comic book this was! The usual range of garish colors had been extended to include metallic gold and copper and silver, worked into the intricate border around the cover and the title.

Georgie rolled the magazine in reverse to flatten it

and turned it around so that he could read the title. *The Power of the Rellard,* it said, in ornate script across the top of the cover.

The room was shocked into absolute stillness. Georgie no longer heard the wind and snow outside the window. The thumping of his heart filled his ears as he sat staring at the magazine lying slightly curled on the desk before him.

Beneath the ornate title was a picture of a huge man with blue wings and white horns, flying through a dreadful stormy sky. In his arms he was carrying a little girl with a withered right arm and hand. Below this figure stood a boy and a girl looking up at the pair in the sky. The boy wore glasses and was plump. The girl was the taller of the two and had long blond hair.

Georgie's fingers were stiff but he forced them to turn the first page of the comic. Adjusting his glasses and leaning hard against the desk, he began to read.

"Georgie, Dad's called you three times for dinner, now come on!" The corners of Shelley's mouth were puckered in exasperation. She stood over the boy, hands on hips.

"What?" she yelped. *"Not* reading a comic? I thought that type of literature was beneath the Big Brain!"

Georgie slapped shut the comic book and clasped it to his chest.

"Nothing!" he gasped. "No one!"

"What?" Shelley leaned forward. "What's the matter?" She narrowed her eyes. "What *is* that magazine?" She grabbed a corner and pulled.

Georgie came up out of the chair, frantically trying to hold on to the comic and push away Shelley's hand at the same time.

"No! No! You'll tear it! Let go!" he pleaded. Across the room they struggled, Shelley pulling at the book, trying to pry Georgie's arms loose from their frantic clasp; Georgie pleading all the while for her to let go, let go, parrying Shelley's attack and trying to protect the magazine. His glasses started to slide down his nose and he put up a hand to save them. Shelley seized the opportunity to swoop in under his guard and wrenched the comic book from his grasp.

"Don't!" pleaded Georgie.

Shelley, grinning triumphantly, held the comic high and read out the title. *Scorpion Man—Terror of the Desert!* The grin faded and she lowered the book to begin flicking through the pages, stopping to read, hurrying on, finally slapping it shut and tossing it to the astounded Georgie.

"You're crazy, getting excited about an ordinary

old comic like that. Scorpion Man, indeed!" And she flounced out the door.

Georgie stumbled after her, comic clasped to his chest, glasses askew.

"You're sure, you're sure it's about Scorpion Man?"

Shelley didn't even deign to answer. She continued down the hallway, calling over her shoulder, "Better get down to dinner before Dad really gets angry."

Georgie held the comic away from his chest, read the cover again. His face paled. He stumbled after Shelley.

"Are you sure? Shelley, please, just have a look. Are you sure you read Scorpion Man?" He was almost blubbering, eyes wide behind the crooked glasses, circling in front of Shelley, stumbling backward, trying to get her to stop, pleading with her to look at the book.

"Young man, you've held up dinner for this family long enough!" Dad's arm suddenly appeared over Georgie's shoulder. "Give that to me!" And he scooped up the comic book.

"Dad! No! Please!" begged Georgie, but his father was adamant and forced the trembling boy to sit down at the table. Mum and Lucy were already seated, eyes wide, and Shelley slid sedately into her chair.

"Now what's so important about this comic?" Dad held it up.

Georgie gulped. "Nothing."

"Nothing? A nothing kept you from your dinner and upset the whole family?"

Georgie nodded, stopped, and then shook his head. "I didn't mean to, I didn't hear you calling, I'm sorry," he mumbled.

"Sorry." Dad's voice was flat. "For months you've been telling us that comics rot the brain and so forth and then you make us wait for our dinner while you engross yourself in this garbage." He held up the comic book between a fastidious thumb and finger and read out in a theatrical voice, "Merboy, the Son of the Sea, unravels the riddles of the deeps!" He looked askance at Georgie. "This is engrossing?"

Georgie's mouth had dropped open.

"Dear, sarcasm doesn't become you. Sit down and eat," said Mum. Dad looked sheepish, dropped the comic on the corner of the table and sat down at his place.

"Just be sure you come when you're called next time," he warned and began to eat.

Shelley stared fiercely at Georgie. She raised her

eyebrows so high they almost disappeared into her hair.

"Merboy?" she mouthed.

Georgie looked sick and shrugged.

Shelley tried again. "Whatever became of Scorpion Man?" she asked. "I thought he was in that comic."

"That's enough, young lady." Dad was firm. "Eat your dinner." He and Mum began to discuss business.

"Just wondered," mumbled Shelley. She couldn't bear not to have the last word.

"Georgie, are you sure you feel all right?" Mum looked from her son's full plate to his flushed face. She was clearing the table before dessert.

"I'm fine." Georgie tried to make his voice sound hearty. "Dieting." He grinned weakly.

"Next time you're dieting tell me before I dish up so that you don't waste good food." His mother wasn't impressed. "Do you want any dessert? It's apple pie."

Georgie said, "Yes, please," but couldn't eat all of that either. The meal ended at last and the three children adjourned to the kitchen. Mum and Dad took their coffee to the living room.

"That comic isn't about any Merboy!" Shelley was dumping the dirty plates into the soap-filled sink. "Here, it's your turn to wash." She handed the dishcloth to Georgie.

"I know." He began to run the cloth around on the surface of a plate.

"Well, why did Dad say that? Look! It's about some guy dressed up like a scorpion." Shelley stood, hip leaning against the sink, flicking through the comic book while she waited for Georgie to wash the plates.

"Is it?"

"Of course it is. I'm looking at it with my very own eyes!" Shelley was indignant. She turned to take a bowl from Lucy. "Honestly, Lucy, you'll never get the table cleared at this rate. Can't you carry more than one dish at a time?"

"Lucy . . . " Georgie's voice was gentle. "You won't drop them. Honest. You're okay to carry two or three at once. Don't pay any attention to her."

"Why shouldn't she pay attention to me?" huffed Shelley. "I'm just trying to help her."

"Not you," said Georgie. He looked at Lucy. "It's Mrs. Gibbs, isn't it?"

Lucy looked long at Georgie and then hung her head.

"What on earth are you on about?" Shelley slapped her tea towel down on the drainboard. "Who is Mrs. Gibbs?"

"Lucy?" Georgie's soft voice insisted. "It's her, isn't it? Mrs. Gibbs?"

Lucy kept her head down and nodded a small nod. When she lifted her eyes to look at Georgie, they were huge and full of tears.

"What am I going to do?" she whispered.

Georgie straightened his shoulders and turned to the astonished Shelley.

"You get the rest of the dishes off the table, quick, and I'll finish here. Lucy, you wipe and Shelley will help. Then we can talk."

"Now," said Georgie. He was seated on his desk chair facing the two girls, who were on his bed. Lucy was hugging her knees and Shelley sat up straight, arms folded. "We all heard Dad say this was called *Merboy, Son of the Sea*. Correct?"

"Right."

Lucy nodded.

"And you," Georgie pointed at Shelley, "say it's about Scorpion Man?"

"Right again."

"Here, have another look."

Shelley took the proffered magazine and flicked through it. "Yep. Scorpion Man, all right. So what is going on?"

Georgie slapped the comic softly against his knee. "When I read it, it's about Rowan, and us. It's called *The Power of the Rellard.*"

Shelley gasped and Lucy slowly unfolded herself.

"Really, Georgie?" she asked. "Is it really about us? Let me see!" and she bounced off the bed. But when she looked at the cover of the comic, her face fell.

"What is it, Lucy?" Georgie leaned forward, voice urgent. "What's the name of the comic?"

"It's just fairy tales." She sagged back against the bed. "Just fairy tales."

"Open it up," encouraged Georgie. "Go on, open it up and have a look."

Listlessly, the girl turned the pages of the comic book. "No, just fairy tales," she said and handed it back to Georgie.

"What's going on, Georgie?" Shelley was excited. "How can a comic change like that?"

"I have an idea," said Georgie, "but we need to conduct one more experiment and get the answer to one more question before I tell you what I think. Now then, Lucy, here's what I want you to do."

A few minutes later, Lucy approached her mother, who was fiercely darning one of Georgie's socks.

"Can you help me with some words?" she asked.

Mum looked up from the puckered toe of the sock and sighed. "Gladly. Words I'm good at. Darning I'm not!"

Lucy pointed to a page in the comic. "That word there," she said.

" 'Munchkin,' " read her mother. " 'The Witch of the East was proud of those silver shoes,' said one of the Munchkins, 'and there is some charm connected with them; but what it is we never knew.' " Mother turned the pages back to read the front of the comic book. "*The Wonderful Wizard of Oz*! One of my all-time favorites. It doesn't seem right, somehow to have it a comic. Let's see, how did they do the Cowardly Lion?" She turned the pages rapidly. "Yes . . . not bad . . . and the Scarecrow . . . pretty much as I imagined it . . . Oh, I'm sorry, Lucy, I've lost your place," and she began flicking back through the magazine.

"That's all right, Mum. I'll find it," and Lucy picked up the comic, tucked it under her arm and leaned over to kiss her mother. "Thank you."

Back in Georgie's bedroom Lucy carefully laid

the comic book on the desk. *"The Wonderful Wizard of Oz,"* she said. "For Mum it's *The Wonderful Wizard of Oz.*"

Before Georgie could comment, Shelley burst through the door.

"Dad found it in the front hall, rolled up against the wall," she puffed. "He thinks it came with the mail."

"Just what I thought," said Georgie. "Now, Lucy. Remember what Rowan said about sending a message to me?"

Lucy nodded. "By way of the slitted brass."

"But this is a comic!" Shelley interrupted. "What does a comic have to do with metal?"

"Think!" ordered Georgie. "Think! How does the mail get into the house?"

"Through the door."

"Through *what* in the door?"

"Through the mail flap—oh!" Shelley clapped her hands to her cheeks. "It's brass. And it has a slot for the mail to slide through. I get it! The mail slot is the slitted brass!"

Georgie nodded. "Just as Rowan promised. The message came through the slitted brass."

"Georgie!" Shelley's curiosity made her fierce. "Tell! What is the message?"

"It's a protected message." Georgie spoke calmly, tapping the comic with his finger. "It's a message for me, and only for me. So when other people read it, the book protects the message and changes the story to something else."

"Yes, yes, yes, I understand that." Shelley gave a little bounce. "But what *is* the message? Get to the message!"

Georgie calmly continued speaking. "For me it is the story of us—of how Lucy earned the Power of the Rellard—from the very beginning, when Mum brought home that old cardboard stage. From the very beginning up to right now." He opened the comic to the last page and quickly scanned it. "Yes," he said as he closed the book. "The story right up to this very moment."

"But it's supposed to be a message, not a story," insisted Shelley.

"The story *is* the message. It was sent so that I could see what's really happening to all of us. To me and to you, Shelley. And you, Lucy."

"Are you sure?" Lucy's voice cracked. "Are you sure it's a message from . . ." She stopped, swallowed, and went on, "From . . . ?"

"From Rowan! Who else!" Georgie smiled.

He got up from his chair and knelt in front of

Lucy. Taking her right hand gently in his, he asked, "Why didn't you tell us, Lucy? Why didn't you tell us about her?"

Lucy burst into tears.

ELEVEN

Lucy Trapped

"I didn't know what to do." Lucy sniffed.

"It's all right, now," Georgie soothed, stroking her hand. "I know what she's been doing to you."

"Who?" insisted Shelley. "You know but I don't! Do you *mind*? Could you *please* enlighten me? Who is this 'she'?"

"Mrs. Gibbs," said Georgie.

"You said her name before, in the kitchen, but who is Mrs. Gibbs? I've never heard of her!"

"Yes, you have." Lucy's voice was firmer. "I told you after Miss Reedy left."

"No you didn't! I don't remember!" bristled Shelley.

"Stop that!" Georgie stood and patted Lucy clumsily on the shoulder. "Tell Shelley what happened, all of it." He sat down at the desk.

"Can't you? It's in the comic book, there." Lucy pointed. "You tell."

"No." Georgie was firm. *"You* have to tell us."

"Part of the message?" Lucy asked.

"Part of the message," agreed Georgie.

"I'm waiting, patiently." Shelley had switched to sarcasm.

"Well," began Lucy, "it was when Mrs. Gibbs made me get up to give my name, the day she first came, after Miss Reedy had left. . . ."

"Ah," said Mrs. Gibbs, in that at-last-I've-found-you! tone of voice. She smiled down at Lucy. "Now what is your name?"

"Lucy."

"Just Lucy? Nothing else?"

Lucy felt giddy. I'm caught, she thought and tried to look away from the woman's dark gaze. She leaned against her desk.

"No."

"No, what?"

"No, not just Lucy."

"Look at me!" the woman ordered. When she held Lucy's gaze fixed in her own, she smiled. It was just a turning up of the lips, that smile. "Now start again. What is your name and how old are you?"

But though she tried hard, Lucy couldn't speak. Her tongue had become thick and wouldn't come away from the roof of her mouth. She moved her lips but nothing came out.

"Well, what do we have here, class? A goldfish?" Mrs. Gibbs spoke in a falsely jolly kind of voice and a couple of the children tittered nervously. She leaned closer. "I do believe it's trying to speak! Come on, now," she cajoled sweetly, "tell us your name and your age. That's not too hard, is it?" She looked around at the rest of the class, playing to them as an actor plays to an audience. "What do *you* think? Name? Age? Not a really difficult thing, is it?"

A couple of children at the back of the room called out, "No!" and Sheryl turned around to stare at Lucy. Without Mrs. Gibbs's dreadful gaze fixed on her, Lucy was able to collect her wits and loosen her tongue. She blurted out her name and age and made a dive for her seat.

"No you don't!" The woman grabbed her right arm and pulled her up again. "I want to know more about the little gaping goldfish girl. Stand up here."

A few more titters. Sheryl looked away.

"Now then, Lucy," Mrs. Gibbs continued, "tell me why you're so old. You're one year older than everyone else in this classroom."

"Miss, it's because . . ." Jeremy tried to explain but was cut short by a curt wave of the woman's hand.

"Quiet! Let *her* explain," she ordered, and folded her arms. "Go on," she said. "Tell us, Lucy."

After a short silence Lucy managed to whisper, "Sick. I was sick."

The woman leaned down, hand behind her ear. "What was that? Don't mumble-grumble in your beard." She smirked at the class, there were more titters and somebody laughed outright.

Lucy swallowed, hard. "I was sick last year," she managed to say in a fairly loud voice.

"She had to repeat." It was Jeremy again. Mrs. Gibbs glared at him.

"So," she said, turning back to Lucy. "Sick, were you? That's a shame."

Lucy looked at the floor.

"Look at me!" thundered the woman. Lucy's head snapped up and the class was suddenly silent, shocked silent.

"What sickness was this?"

Lucy shook her head.

"You don't know?"

Lucy nodded.

The woman leaned down, putting her face so close that Lucy could see the pores in her skin. "This sickness, did it leave any mark on you, any sign that it had been in your body?"

Lucy nodded, after a long pause.

"I see." Mrs. Gibbs straightened. "Well, class, this is very interesting. A sickness that leaves a mark." She paused, and then went on. "Lucy, show me the mark left by the sickness."

Lucy shuddered, and across the room Joey began to sniffle.

"Show me, Lucy," said Mrs. Gibbs. "You are going to show me even if we have to stand here all day before you do it. So let's not keep the rest of the class waiting. Just show me the mark of the sickness!"

Lucy slowly extended her right arm. From shoulder to elbow, it was firm and round, still lightly tanned from the summer sun. But below the elbow, the arm was shrunken and twisted, the wrist bony and awkward. The hand was small, wizened, the fingers tangled.

"Lift it higher, Lucy," demanded Mrs. Gibbs. "Higher!"

Lucy struggled to lift the arm, trembling with the effort.

"Higher! Higher!" urged the woman.

It seemed to Lucy that all the class were chanting with the woman, gleefully screaming, "Higher! Higher!" as she struggled to lift the arm. Perspiration broke out on her forehead, she strained to lift the withered, shrunken, ugly arm high, higher. Tears started from her eyes and rolled down her cheeks.

"Higher!" The woman was shouting, eyes wide and gleaming. "Higher!"

At last the arm was almost straight up and Mrs. Gibbs gripped it around the wrist. Lucy felt as if she were dangling from the woman's grasp.

"See class! See! This is the mark left by Lucy's illness!" She turned Lucy around so that all the children in the class could see the arm. Gasps, titters, snickers, and a faint clapping from the back of the room.

Mrs. Gibbs flung the arm away from her and Lucy staggered back against her desk.

"Sit down," the woman ordered and moved on to the next child.

Lucy was trembling so violently that she could hardly stay in her seat. Her arm hurt, her wrist smarted, the hand throbbed where it had struck the desk when Mrs. Gibbs flung it away. She folded it close, hugging it with her good strong arm and leaned her forehead on her desk. Her ears rang.

"Beware the lifted hand," she whispered. "Beware the lifted hand!"

"What does that mean?" interrupted Shelley. "Beware the lifted hand?"

Lucy told of the message she heard as she lay on the newly cut stump of the Big Tree. "It was Rowan, warning me. I tried to tell you but you were asleep. And the next day school started and Suzanne and all and you stopped listening about Rowan."

"That's not true, I would have listened!" Shelley protested.

"You didn't!" Lucy insisted. "I tried!"

"But Mum and Dad? Why didn't you tell them about Mrs. Gibbs?"

"I was afraid! I couldn't!"

"But that's silly."

"Shelley, if you want to know what has been happening to Lucy, you are going to have to be quiet!" Georgie adjusted his glasses and looked at Lucy. Shelley gave a token snort of rebellion and settled down to listen.

"I didn't know what to do," continued Lucy. "I was so scared."

For a time after the arm-raising episode, Mrs. Gibbs

ignored Lucy. She quickly finished hearing the names of the rest of the class, and launched directly into math. Papers were handed down the rows of seats.

"Just a review," said Mrs. Gibbs.

Lucy managed to lift her head and focus on the figures on the paper. But it was difficult to stop trembling and her awkward left hand could not be made to hold the pencil. It slipped out of her grasp, rolled down the desk, and bounced onto the floor.

Lucy darted a look to the front of the room. Mrs. Gibbs had her back turned. Slowly, Lucy reached down and retrieved the pencil. Her heart sank. The lead was broken!

To sharpen it, she would have to get up and go to the back of the room where the pencil sharpener was mounted on the top of the science cupboard. The woman would look at her and Lucy didn't want that. She couldn't bear that! She held the pencil in her lap and leaned weakly against the hard edge of the desk. What was she to do?

"Just a few more minutes, class." Mrs. Gibbs lifted her head to look around the room. Quickly Lucy bowed her head and pretended to be writing with the broken pencil. At least she would be safe for a few more minutes!

When the teacher collected the papers and picked up Lucy's almost blank page, she made a disgusted sound in her throat.

"Well, children," she said. "The mysterious disease seems to have emptied little Goldfish Girl's head, too."

Lucy's ears burned and she stared at the top of her desk. Please, her silent thoughts begged, please go away. Please leave me alone.

"I will not go away," Mrs. Gibbs said. Shocked to hear her unspoken thoughts voiced by this woman, Lucy lifted her head and looked at the teacher. She was smiling a one-sided smile, a bad smile, Lucy was to describe it later to Georgie and Shelley.

"But I can help you to be alone, gladly." She turned to the rest of the class. "I think that's the least we should do, don't you? Help her to be alone, if that's what she wants?"

The children stared blankly at Mrs. Gibbs.

"Now then, little gasping Goldfish Girl," the woman continued. "Stand up and move your seat and desk to that corner. You can be alone there."

Lucy struggled to her feet and awkwardly hauled and shoved her desk and seat out of its position in the row, down the aisle and over to the corner. Mrs. Gibbs walked along with her, giving directions and making encouraging comments, but making no move to assist the struggling girl. And she did not allow anyone else to help Lucy. Jeremy put out an arm to help shove when Lucy's desk got caught up against his own, but the teacher stopped him.

"Let her do it on her own!" she snapped. "If she wants to be alone, let her manage it for herself."

At last the desk was in place and Lucy sank into the seat. Her arm hurt and she was breathless with the humiliation of the struggle. From this position, she could see only the flag and Mrs. Gibbs's desk. The rest of the class was behind her.

I can't bear this, she thought, but caught the thought back when she saw Mrs. Gibbs looking at her.

The woman smiled her peculiar smile. "You'll just have to bear up, won't you?" she remarked, and Lucy's heart sank. It was obvious that her mind was open to this woman, that she could read Lucy's mind as easily as Lucy herself could listen to Joey's thoughts.

At this point, Shelley could not contain herself.

"Joey's thoughts? Could you hear them?" she exclaimed, and Lucy had to stop in the middle of her account of the first day with Mrs. Gibbs and explain how she could tune in on some people's thoughts.

"Mine? Can you do it with mine?" Shelley's eyes were wide.

Lucy shook her head. "I don't know. I never tried it with you."

"But just think how marvelous that would be! Why didn't you try with us? I would have!" Shelley bounced on the bed. "I couldn't have stopped myself!"

Lucy shrugged. "You're my sister," she explained lamely.

Shelley sat up straight. "I'll have to write it in the notebook—about the mind-reading. That must be another way you can use the Power."

"I thought you didn't know where the book was?" Shelley just looked blankly at Lucy.

"Go on about Mrs. Gibbs," encouraged Georgie.

"The rest of the day was more of the same," said Lucy.

Lucy could not seem to do anything correctly. Her pencil lead broke again and again. Her eraser rolled under the book cupboard and she was afraid to retrieve it. Mrs. Gibbs showed all the class her messy spelling paper with the crossed-out words. Her thoughts were so rattled that she could not follow along in the story they were all reading and everyone laughed when Mrs. Gibbs asked where her little mind was.

Joey sought her out at lunchtime and they sat hunched together over their sandwiches, both so miserable and frightened that they were no help for each other.

The day finally ended. Lucy cleared her desk along with the rest of the class, scrabbling her pencil and ruler into the desk, closing the lid, sitting up straight, eyes ahead, hands folded on the desk, ready to be dismissed.

She had decided that she would wait for Carrie on the corner. She didn't care how cold it was; she couldn't spend another minute here in this room, here with this woman. Lucy stiffened her spine and stared straight ahead, willing her mind blank. She *had* to get out of here.

She kept her back straight but her spirits sagged as everyone, every single child, was dismissed except her. The rest of the class clattered out to the hall-way, where they began to pull on their boots and heavy coats, noisily searching out gloves and scarves and caps. Lucy was left alone, behind the hanging folds of the flag, hands on desk, eyes straight ahead, trying desperately not to think about Carrie.

Out of the corner of her eye she could see the teacher walking slowly across the room toward her. At last the woman stood next to her and spoke softly.

"Now you and I will have this time together, this small half of an hour," she gloated.

Lucy's scalp prickled, but she kept her eyes focused on the folds of the flag. "May I please be dismissed," she asked, holding in her mind a picture of her coat and boots waiting for her in the hallway, of the door opening at the end of the hall.

The teacher laughed. "You'll don your little boots and the coat in the half of an hour," she promised. "I have been looking forward to this time with you for all the day. Miss Reedy wrote about it in her plan book, so kind she was. Yes, child, I have been waiting a long time to be alone with you."

Lucy's heart fluttered and her mind filled with a fog of despair.

"Go on! What did she say then?" Shelley leaned forward.

"I don't know!" Lucy answered. "I don't remember."

"Think!" insisted Shelley. "You must be able to remember what she did. You must!"

Lucy's chin set stubbornly. "I can't. I've tried. I only start remembering when Carrie came in to get me."

"Carrie!" Shelley was getting more and more excited. "Why didn't you tell her right then about the teacher? She's being paid to look after you."

"I couldn't," Lucy said. "I just couldn't."

"It's beyond me how you could just let this horrible woman be so mean to you and not say anything to anybody!" Shelley was almost shouting at Lucy in her exasperation. "You just let her!"

Lucy hunched her shoulders and looked pleadingly at Georgie, who nodded and picked up the comic from the desk.

"I can tell you what happened," he said, and opening the book he began to read to the girls.

TWELVE

An Attack Is Planned

Georgie finished reading, closed the comic carefully, and laid it face-down on the desk. The three children sat for a moment in silence.

"Hypnotizing you. That's what she's been doing. How long?"

Lucy thought a moment. "A lot of weeks, I think."

Shelley shook her head in amazement. "Weeks! And to think that none of us noticed the change in you."

"We weren't supposed to notice," said Georgie. "We were all looking somewhere else."

"I just thought . . ." Lucy stopped, swallowed and plunged on. "I thought you just didn't care . . . about me, and the Power. I thought I was stupid and awful and weak and a . . . a *cripple!*" She hugged her arm and looked at the floor.

Georgie leaned forward. "Lucy, every day in that half an hour after school, Mrs. Gibbs tried to get you to tell her about the Power of the Rellard. She tried every way she knew how. But"—Georgie stood and spread his arms wide—"*but*, you didn't tell her! That's great!"

Lucy lifted her head. Georgie began to pace in a small circle on the floor between his desk and the bed.

"So, what was she to do? She did the next best thing. She took away your belief in the Power of the Rellard by making you think that you're just a stupid, silly little girl with a crippled arm."

"And none of us noticed." Shelley shook her head.

"I didn't read it all." Georgie sat down at the desk and picked up the comic book. "I didn't read the part that tells how the rest of us were kind of . . ." Georgie tilted his head back, searching for the right word, "sort of, well, *enchanted,* yes, enchanted so that we didn't notice how Lucy has been getting sadder and weaker and kind of just . . . well, just disappearing."

"Enchanted?" Lucy moved closer to Shelley. "Like by a wicked witch?" Her eyes were huge.

Shelley put her arm around Lucy.

"That's right." Georgie nodded and lowered his voice. "Things are really working along now. The bad ones are coming out in the open. They're showing their hand. They want the Power! That's the message from Rowan!"

"What things?" demanded Shelley. "Who? Who are they?"

"Mrs. Gibbs is one," whispered Lucy. "She's really bad!"

"But who else?" Shelley pointed at the comic. "Did he tell you, Georgie? Did Rowan tell you?"

"Who has kept us so occupied that we've completely forgotten about the Power of the Rellard and haven't noticed what's been happening to Lucy right under our noses?" Georgie lifted his hands and his eyebrows, questioning. "*Who* has done that?"

"No games, Georgie. Tell us." Shelley was grim.

Georgie dropped his hands and his eyebrows slid down behind his glasses. "Mr. Boaz. And Susie Q."

Shelley's mouth dropped open in astonishment. "Suzanne? She's just a girl! Like me! And Mr. Boaz is a teacher!"

"So is Mrs. Gibbs!"

Shelley shut her mouth with a snap.

"And," Georgie folded his arms, "the new photographer, the one that's cut all his prices and messed up Dad's business."

"The new photographer!" Shelley's voice rose.

"Do you have to repeat everything?" Georgie was disgusted. "Can't you just listen and think?"

Shelley folded her arms and glared. Then she took a deep breath and spoke in a low, controlled voice. "Georgie, listen to me. I know you think you have had a message from Rowan . . ."

"He said he'd send a message to you," interrupted Lucy. "And don't forget the blue feather!"

Shelley dismissed the blue feather with a wave of her hand. "Whatever he said, it all sounds crazy to me. How can ordinary people—like Suzanne, and that photographer—how can they be mixed up in magic and the Power of the Rellard?"

"Do you want fairies and goblins and witches?" Georgie's glasses glinted in the light of the desk lamp. "How long do you think someone in a black pointy hat would last in a classroom? Or in the marching band?"

"The bad ones have made themselves look just like us," Lucy asserted.

"Right!" Georgie jumped up and paced back and forth. "Now, if an evil-looking wizard with warts and a long gray beard came along and tried to get me to listen to him, I'd be suspicious! Right?" Shelley nodded.

"Right!" Lucy bounced on the bed.

"But!" Georgie held up an admonitory finger. "But, what if a teacher, a *science* teacher, came along and told me how smart I was and got me so interested in doing things that I didn't *notice* anything else? I wouldn't be suspicious at all! Would I?"

"No! No! No!" Lucy bounced higher.

"And that's exactly what happened with Mr. Boaz!" Georgie dropped his hand.

"All those expeditions and experiments and projects, is that how he did it?" Shelley asked.

"Yes!" Georgie nodded. "And he kept saying I was very intelligent, too intelligent for . . ." Georgie stopped, his face flushed a dull red.

"For what?" prodded Shelley.

"You *are* clever, Georgie," Lucy spoke into the silence. "You *are* cleverer than me, and Shelley, too."

"That's what he said, only he made it awful, didn't he?" asked Shelley.

Georgie sat down on the chair and leaned his elbows on his knees. He clasped his hands tightly and spoke to them. "Yes. He said I was . . . that I was very intelligent, more intelligent than the rest of my family, that they couldn't understand my mind, couldn't appreciate me. It was like maybe I didn't really belong in this family . . ."

"Just like Mrs. Gibbs," said Lucy. "Only she said I was too stupid. She said I couldn't learn and that you all hated me for being stupid and . . ." here she looked down at her hand.

Shelley made a comforting noise in her throat and smiled at Lucy.

"And," Lucy continued, "she said I should be sent away!"

"Lucy!" Shelley was shocked.

"She did! She said she was going to send a note. A note to Mum and Dad. A note to tell them to send me away."

"Oh, Lucy, how awful."

"Yes." Lucy nodded. "She was going to send that note!"

"But Mum and Dad wouldn't believe her!" protested Shelley.

"She's grown up! And a teacher!" cried Lucy.

"And Lucy hasn't been doing any real work at school," Georgie said. "The comic told that."

"I can't," pleaded Lucy. "She gets me so upset, I can't remember anything!"

"We know now," said Georgie. "We'll protect you, Lucy. You won't be sent away."

"And the photographer, the new one? Is he one of

the bad ones, too?" Shelley asked.

"If he hadn't come to town, Dad wouldn't need to have Mum working at the studio and she would be home, not so busy and worried, and she would have noticed that something was wrong with Lucy."

"And Dad's heart trouble. Did the bad ones send the heart trouble?"

"It didn't say in the book, but I'm sure they caused it," said Georgie. "Do you see, Shelley? Do you see how they worked it?"

"Yes, I can see all that," agreed Shelley. She opened her mouth to go on but after a pause, shut it tight. She lifted her chin stubbornly and glared at Georgie.

"Go on, Shelley. Who else?"

She shook her head.

"Shelley, you know that Suzanne . . ."

But Shelley wouldn't let Georgie continue. "No! No! You don't understand! She's my friend, my best friend! I've never had one before! She likes me. She's not a bad one, not Suzanne!" She began to cry.

Georgie looked sad. "How do you think I feel about Mr. Boaz?" he asked.

Shelley sniffed and wiped her eyes on a corner of the bedspread. "I don't know. I don't care. You're clever, anyway. Everyone knows that. But I haven't got anything like that."

"But you're musical! Just like Mum!" insisted Lucy.

"What has she got from her music? She can't even play a whole piece through anymore!" Shelley said, a bitter undertone creeping into her voice. "So what good is music?"

"So what did Suzanne do for you?" Georgie leaned back against the desk.

"*You* know, smarty! You've read it in the book from Rowan!" Shelley's eyes blazed.

"Tell us," ordered Georgie. "Go on, tell us about Suzanne."

Shelley sniffed and looked long at her brother. "A friend," she said, flatly. "She is my best friend."

Shelley always hoped that each year school would be different, that this year she would have a friend, a best friend. She dreamed that this friend would be one of that small select group in her class whom everyone admired, who did exciting things and laughed and sparkled and succeeded and were popular. But so far, she had never had such a friend. She was a quiet girl at school, doing her work neatly, promptly and very well, reading books and being musical. Her two best friends and companions had always been Georgie and Lucy, a fact which made her feel slightly ashamed.

But this year had been different! The first day, Shelley had gone to school with her mind totally occupied with the wonder of the silhouette on the tree stump. She planned to go to the library after school and look up things about flowers. They would have a language or a symbolism, she felt sure. She would ask Miss Marks to help her. She so wanted to receive a special communication from Rowan!

"We're part of something important—something wonderful!" she thought, as she yanked open the heavy door that led to her area of the school. She already had her locker number and key and walked along checking the numbers at the top of the lockers.

"Fifty-four, fifty-five . . . must be around the corner," she thought, and turned right. That was when she first saw Suzanne.

Some girls were standing in the middle of the hallway, chattering, laughing, stroking back bright strands of hair, shifting their necks, shoulders, laughing, sparkling in the sunlight that fell from a high window.

Shelley, glancing at them from the numbers of the

lockers, stopped absolutely still when she saw the girl who was the center of the group's attention.

"Golden!" was the word that flashed into her mind. And ever after, she thought of Suzanne as golden, even after she really knew her, really saw her; even then, she was a golden image in Shelley's mind.

"Hi!" the golden girl called. "My name's Suzanne. What's yours?"

So simply, so easily, Suzanne had captured Shelley.

Suzanne and Shelley were in the same class for the first period, and it was only natural that they should walk there together. For Shelley, it was a new experience. She had not always walked the school hallways alone, but she had never walked with anyone who attracted as much attention as Suzanne. The girl seemed to glow. Heads turned, eyes swiveled. Suzanne spread smiles and hellos with lavish abandon and was rewarded with instant attention and appreciation. Somehow, Suzanne made Shelley feel that she was included, that she, too, was being smiled at, noticed, appreciated.

And it didn't end when the bell rang at the end of first period. Suzanne bent her golden head over her timetable and declared herself totally unable to find her way without Shelley, and when lunchtime came, it was Shelley she drew to her side.

"Come home with me after school. I'll show you my scrapbook and we can listen to records," she promised. Shelley protested weakly that she had to practice her piano lesson and there was something else she had meant to do. But Suzanne insisted prettily, blue eyes wide, and Shelley smiled back at her.

"Yes," she said, heart tripping with happiness, "yes, I would love to hear your records, yes, yes!"

After that, they were best friends and everyone knew it. Every spare moment of Shelley's life was filled with Suzanne.

"No one has ever been my best friend. No one." Shelley set her chin firmly. "She's not like Mr. Boaz or Mrs. Gibbs. She's not anything to do with the Power of the Rellard! She really likes me. I don't care what your old comic says!" Shelley got up and walked stiffly to the door, where she turned. "I'm going to my room to look for the Rellard notebook," she announced, looking at neither of them. The Do Not Disturb sign swung wildly from the knob as she went out.

"Did Rowan say what to do next?" asked Lucy.

Georgie shook his head. "No. It's really up to

Shelley now, according to the story. But she's not going to be much use if she can't see that Suzanne is one of the bad ones."

Lucy agreed. "But you can't blame her. She's been really popular since Suzanne came, and she likes that."

"She'll still have friends without Suzanne," said Georgie. "Just like I'm still intelligent without Mr. Boaz."

"She doesn't think so," said Lucy, hugging her knees.

When Shelley returned with the notebook, she made Lucy go back and describe just how she had listened to the thoughts of the other children in the class, and she wrote it all down in her neat, careful writing.

"You've only done it at school, with the other kids?" Shelley questioned Lucy. "Not here at home? Not with Georgie or me?"

Lucy shook her head.

"How about with Mrs. Gibbs?"

Lucy shivered. "She does it to me. I told you."

"Yes, I know." Shelley tapped her teeth with her pencil. "But it seems to me that it's time that you went on the offensive and tried to read *her* mind."

"She's big and powerful," Lucy protested. "I'm

scared of her. I don't *want* to know what she is thinking!"

"We have to stop Mrs. Gibbs, and you're the only one who can do it." Shelley snapped the notebook shut. "If you don't listen to her thoughts, you won't know what she plans to do with the Power of the Rellard."

"And if we know what she wants to do with it, we'll know what we have to do to stop her and the others," Georgie went on.

Lucy shrank down. "I'm scared! She's awful! You don't know!"

"I'll come for you after school from now on." Shelley's finger traced around the drawing of the Rellard man on the front of the notebook. "That way you won't have to stay with her for that extra half an hour."

"But what about your music . . . and Suzanne?"

"Well, this will be a good test for Suzanne. Won't it?" Shelley's chin lifted. "She'll understand. I'll prove that she's not a bad one."

"Oh, thank you, Shelley!"

Shelley's finger stopped and she grabbed up the notebook with both hands. "The Rellard man!" she exclaimed. "Have you used him on Mrs. Gibbs?"

Lucy shook her head. "I took him off," she said.

"I put him away. He didn't seem real anymore."

"Get him!" Shelley ordered. "I've got an idea."

"Now then," Shelley continued, when the little dough medallion was hanging around Lucy's neck once more, "when we go back to school, here is what we are going to do. . . ."

THIRTEEN

Shelley Meets the Real Suzanne

The day after Georgie deciphered the comic-book message, a snowstorm hit the area and all roads became impassable. The children were unable to go outdoors for three days and then, when they did, they were greeted by a completely white world, frozen under a high, wind-driven blanket of snow.

The snowplows could only open a few roads and Dad was worried that business would be affected. It was. Few people braved the cold and the snow and Mum looked grim.

The short respite was broken by another winter storm that howled and blasted its way through two freezing days.

"I've never seen storms like this." Dad shook his

head. "What's the reading on the thermometer in your weather station, Georgie?" But the thermometer was buried under the snow.

Dad checked the central heating system. Then, despite the wind and the rushing curtain of snow, he insisted on making his way out to the woodpile and carrying in armload after armload of wood. Mum and Georgie helped with the carrying, while Shelley and Lucy knocked off the snow and piled the logs neatly on newspapers in the corner of the kitchen. Afterwards, Dad's face looked gray and tired and their mother's eyes were taut with worry. She scolded him, but he shook his head.

"If this storm keeps up we'll need that wood," he said.

And he was right. The very next day, in the afternoon, the electricity failed. The comforting hum of the central heating died, the lights flicked off, and the refrigerator rattled to silence. The wind rose and swept around the house, sending in little tendrils of cold to creep around their ankles.

"Into the living room, everyone," ordered Mum, and they retreated to the small warm area in front of the fireplace where the wood from the Big Tree crackled and threw out a heartening glow. They wrapped themselves in blankets and toasted bread and marshmallows. Mum made cocoa over the fire and heated soup for their evening meal.

"The electricity will be back on soon," Dad assured them and they slept happily on the mattresses dragged down from their beds, by the warm red coals of the fire.

But it took a week for the electricity to come on. Mum wouldn't allow Dad to carry any more wood, because of his heart, but Shelley and Georgie heaved load after load into the house, and Mum herself carried more than anyone. Lucy was in charge of stacking the logs. They became more adept at cooking over the fire after Mum searched around in the cellar and dragged out the camping gear. They were careful always to leave one tap running slowly so that the waterpipes wouldn't freeze. They read and ate by the light of the lantern until the kerosene ran out, listened to their battery-powered radio, and watched the snow creep up the windows.

On the last day of the holidays the storm abated. Just before noon there was a knock and Carrie tumbled into the front hallway with the news that all schools were closed until the roads could be cleared.

"I suppose you've heard it on the radio but I thought I'd just check." She blew on her fingers and held them to the fire.

"What's it like outside?" Shelley asked.

"Cold!" Carrie grinned. "And the snow! I've never seen so much snow!"

Mum bundled them into extra scarves and caps when Georgie pleaded to go out.

"Goodness knows you need the fresh air," she said.

The weak sunlight on the snow blinded them at first. They pulled their caps down low and squinted against the glare.

"Wow!" said Georgie.

The familiar landscape of their garden was transformed. Low bushes and shrubs were buried under the sweep of the snow. Evergreens had become snowy mounds and the bare trees raised ice and snow-laden branches from deep drifts. The Carney house had a huge shouldering of white up to the eaves and their shed had disappeared except for the roof. There were no roads, no fences, nothing but cold and snow and a vast chill silence blanketing the whole scene.

"This is strange." Georgie had found the snow too dry and powdery for a snowball and he was shaking the glittering white off his mittens.

Carrie agreed. "Weird. Too cold. Too much snow."

"How's your firewood holding out?" Shelley asked.

"Fine. Yours okay?"

"Yes. Dad says we've got enough for another week and then we start on the furniture."

Carrie smiled. "My dad says he's going to start throwing the boys out one by one. They're getting on his nerves."

"Carrie." Shelley was flapping her arms to keep warm. I can pick up Lucy after school from now on. Is that okay with you?"

"Sure." Carrie started flapping her arms, too. The sun was dimmer and a slow cold wind was rising. "I think that's a good idea."

"I know Mother pays you," Shelley went on.

"The money's not important." Carrie slapped her mittens together. "I was going to talk to you about it anyway."

"Why?" Georgie and Lucy huddled close together.

Carrie gave Lucy a hard look. "She's been giving you a bad time, hasn't she? That Mrs. Gibbs?"

Lucy nodded.

"I was afraid of that. I can't do anything about it. So I wanted to talk to you two about it. You need to do something."

Shelley nodded. "Yes. We have a plan."

"Good!" Carrie started toward her house. "And you'd better start thinking about all this, too." She waved an arm at the snow-covered landscape.

"What do you mean?" Lucy called.

Carrie turned and lifted her arms. "All this. It's in your hand, Lucy. I know. I saw you in the tree, remember? It's in your hand," and she disappeared behind the huge snowbank that lined the Carneys' driveway.

"I think she's given us an important clue," said Shelley.

Georgie agreed. "Only how she knows anything about it I can't work out."

"What? What clue?" asked Lucy.

"The cold and the snow. The Power of the Rellard may have been given so that you could save us from the cold and the snow."

"What do you think, Lucy?"

Lucy frowned. "I don't know. I just don't know."

"Well, until you do know or until Rowan sends another message, we'll have to use my plan to find out about the Power from Mrs. Gibbs," said Shelley. "I think she can tell us a lot."

When they went back into the house, the electricity was on again.

Two days later school reopened.

"Now don't forget to wear the Rellard medallion under your shirt," Shelley instructed Lucy as they were bundling up for the cold.

"I won't."

"And don't try any mind-reading until I get there."

"Okay! Okay!"

"I have to be there when you do it."

Lucy nodded.

"I'll be there about five minutes after the last bell rings. It'll take me that long to walk over. Don't panic if she does the hypnotizing again."

"I never panic!" Lucy protested.

"Good! We'll get her!"

"Hey, Shelley!" Suzanne's voice rang across the snow-covered schoolyard.

Shelley warmed to Suzanne's bright smile. "What! What! Tell me what!" she sang.

"Don't make fun of me." Suzanne laughed. "I can't tell you what now! Come home with me after school. I've got so much to tell you. And just wait till you see what I've got to show you!"

Their boots skated on the icy path and their

breath hung in chilly clouds before their faces. It was still dreadfully cold, despite the thin sunlight.

"I can't come home with you. Tell me at lunchtime?"

"Lunchtime isn't long enough. Please, come home with me. I've got something special for you!"

"I can't Suzanne, I really can't. I am going to pick up Lucy after school. I have to help her."

"Lucy!" Suzanne's voice lost a shade of brightness. "Well, that's okay, take her home and leave her and then come on to my house. Hey, maybe you could stay overnight!"

"Mother doesn't want Lucy home alone after school."

"What's happened to Carrie?"

"Nothing's happened to Carrie. Look, Suzanne, I just have this important thing to do with Lucy after school. Today. Maybe I can come home with you tomorrow."

Suzanne tossed her bright head. "Tomorrow may be too late," she said, and ducking into a laughing group nearby, she was swept away down the hall. Shelley stood at her locker, scarf in hand, and gazed thoughtfully after her.

"Darn you, Georgie," she muttered, slinging her boots into the bottom of the locker.

The rest of the day Suzanne swung between begging prettily and threatening lightly. At lunch she sat close to Shelley and told her how much she had missed her during the cold storms. She had a present for Shelley but the weather had been so dreadful, her mother wouldn't let her out to deliver it during the holiday.

"It is such a good present for you, I hope you like it! I just can't wait until you see it!" Suzanne chortled.

When Shelley continued to refuse the after-school invitation, Suzanne glowered and flounced off.

The last class was PE, and as she was hurriedly changing afterward, Shelley heard Suzanne's voice on the other side of the partition that ran down the center of the dressing room.

"Come home with me. We'll listen to records."

Shelley didn't recognize the voice of the girl who replied. "What about Shelley? Isn't she your best friend?"

"What *about* Shelley?" Suzanne's voice was sharp. "She's busy with that little crip of a sister today."

Shelley stood frozen, her head halfway through the neck of her sweater. She was astounded at the tone of Suzanne's voice. And that word! Crip!

Yanking her sweater on, Shelley grabbed her gym gear and ran past the empty bench and around the partition.

"What did you say?" Shelley rushed up to the two girls. "What did you say, Suzanne?"

Suzanne swung around, and when she saw Shelley her mouth hardened and her eyes grew dark.

"You obviously heard me already." She turned to the other girl. "Come on. It's getting crowded in here."

Shelley was trembling with rage and something else. Did this mean that Georgie was right? She had to know. She grabbed Suzanne's arm. "No! Say it! Say it to my face!"

Suzanne turned and faced her. "Okay. Crip! Your little sister Lucy is a cripple!"

Shelley dropped her arm and stood back. She had never seen Suzanne look like this, never. She was still the glowing girl but it was now a steely gleam of malice—cold, bitter, and mean.

"And she's a retard!"

"No!" Shelley was shaking her head.

"Yes! Yes! Retard and crip!" Suzanne moved toward Shelley, bringing her face up close. Shelley could see the dark pupils expanding in Suzanne's eyes.

"She ought to be put away. Crips like her shouldn't be in with normal kids. It makes them sick!"

"Suzanne! She's my sister! Lucy's my sister! She's not . . ."

Suzanne interrupted. "I know exactly who she is!" She stopped, narrowing her eyes. Then she went on. "I've heard all about her, how disgusting she is." She turned and linked arms with the other girl, walking away with her, leaving Shelley rooted in astonishment and rage.

"My aunt is her teacher. She told me all about Lucy, the crip," Suzanne threw over her shoulder. "You'd be surprised at all she's told me." The two girls went out the door.

But just before the door closed, Suzanne turned and shot a look at Shelley, a look that shocked Shelley more than all the bitter, cruel words the girl had flung at her. It was an old look—old and dead and evil.

"Evil!" Shelley shook her head, tried to push the word out of her mind. "Evil!" The word did not belong, not here, ordinary Monday after PE class in the girls' dressing room that reeked of disinfectant, old gym shoes, sweat, and soap. Shelley shivered.

"Evil!" That was a word from fairy stories or the Bible.

"Evil!" Shelley whispered the word. She had seen it, felt it in Suzanne's dark look—the look thrown deliberately down the length of the empty dressing room, freezing her to the spot, locking her in time.

Suddenly the image of Lucy blazed in Shelley's mind. Lucy! And free again, she ran—ran gasping out the door, through the echoing hallway to her locker.

Late! I'll be late! What had happened to the time? Shelley wrenched open her locker and grabbed her coat. Stuffing mittens and scarf in her pockets, she plunged down the short side hallway that led to the outside door.

But it was locked! The door was locked, the chain and padlock tightly gripping the handles that opened the door.

The time! What had happened to the time? This door was open until five!

"Lucy!" Shelley sobbed under her breath. "Lucy, I must get to Lucy." How long had she stood frozen in Suzanne's dark look while time passed; while Lucy faced that woman alone, unprotected except for the little dough medallion?

Shelley raced back up the short hallway and

looked wildly to left and right. She had never been in the building this late before. Surely somewhere there was a door that would release her?

Shelley ran. First to the right, along the darkening corridor. The door at its end was chained and padlocked.

"Oh, no!" she sobbed and ran on. "Help! Please!" she cried as she clattered through the empty, echoing passages lined with locked classroom doors.

"Windows!" she thought. "I'll break a window!" But there were no windows here, and in the next hallway the windows were too high and barred with thick wire mesh.

"Oh, please!" Shelley sobbed. "Oh, please!"

There! She stopped and leaned panting against a row of lockers. She looked wildly around. She heard it again! A whistle! Someone was here, with her! Someone who could help her!

"Help!" she cried. "Help me! Please! I can't get out!"

The distant whistling stopped and down at the far end of the dark corridor there appeared a figure silhouetted against the dim light coming through the heavy glass doors. It looked like the silhouette she had seen on the stump, wings spread, horns rising above the head.

"Rowan!" she shouted, and ran toward the figure.

But it must have been a trick of the light, because in the end she stumbled sobbing and crying into arms that smelled of grease and chalk dust. Mr. Nelson, the school caretaker, patted her shoulder and scolded her for being in the building so late.

"You're not allowed here now!" he chided. Grumbling and muttering the whole way, he led Shelley back to the first door and unlocked the padlock. Shelley was out the door before he had finished loosening the chain and it rattled through the handle.

"Here! Watch out!" Mr. Nelson yelled, but Shelley tore off, out into the darkening winter afternoon, slipping and sliding across the snowy grounds toward the low brick building, where one set of windows glowed brightly.

"Lucy!" she called. "I'm coming!"

FOURTEEN

The Raised Hand Strikes

School that day had felt good to Lucy, she didn't know why. Maybe it was the little lumpy medallion under her sweater, or perhaps the thought that today, after the last bell, she would not have to face Mrs. Gibbs alone. Whatever the reason, she had been able to cope with almost everything, giving Mrs. Gibbs no reason to point out her deficiencies to the rest of the class.

Lucy, when it was her turn, read a whole page aloud with no mistakes. Even better, her recalcitrant left hand suddenly decided to respond to her efforts and produced a page of legible writing. *And,* she missed only two of the multiplication problems!

Not bad, she thought and smiled to herself. She even hummed a little tune as she colored in her basic foods chart, pressing hard on the orange crayon so as to get a thick coating of color on the fruit. All through the long morning Lucy concentrated very hard on her work. She remembered Shelley's warning and closed her mind to Mrs. Gibbs, focusing on the tasks before her.

At lunchtime Sheryl and Joey and Lucy sat together. Sheryl had a new baby brother and was eager to tell Lucy about him. Joey was excited about the model plane he had received for his birthday and rattled on happily. He even invited Lucy over to see the plane, and was so surprised when Lucy said yes, she'd come to his house, that he almost burst into tears. While he sat behind his peanut butter sandwich, trying to collect himself, Sheryl piped up.

"Mrs. Gibbs sent a congraterlations card to us about our new baby."

"She did?" Lucy was surprised.

"Yes, she did." Sheryl daintily lifted the top of her sandwich and inspected the filling, then squashed the top firmly down again.

"My mother says she's the best teacher we've ever had," she announced and took a huge bite.

Lucy's jaw dropped in astonishment and she saw her feelings mirrored on Joey's face. Mrs. Gibbs? The best teacher they'd ever had?

"But she's so mean!" blurted Joey.

"No, she's not. She's not mean at all. I like her," Sheryl protested.

"But what about Lucy?" Joey insisted, pink with indignation. "She was really mean to Lucy. Remember what she did to her, that day?"

"Lucy?" Sheryl looked puzzled. "I don't remember anything mean to Lucy."

"The hand!" Joey lifted his own right hand, in which he was firmly clutching his sandwich. "She made her raise her hand! You remember!"

Sheryl looked blank. "Hand?" Then her face cleared. "But that was Lucy. She raised her hand and asked to be moved." She turned to Lucy. "I don't know why you want to sit over in that corner like that for." She chewed a moment, swallowed, and went on. "Mrs. Gibbs said you probably feel different because of your arm and everything." The last bit of fruit juice chortled up through her straw and she surveyed her empty lunch box. "I'm allowed in the room now. Special duties. Mrs. Gibbs said," and away she went.

Joey and Lucy stared after her.

"I don't get it." Joey frowned mightily. "Mrs. Gibbs *is* mean, isn't she, Lucy?"

Lucy nodded.

"Then why doesn't Sheryl think so?"

"I don't know," Lucy answered.

"It's stupid," grumbled Joey and the two sat quietly munching, both deep in thought.

Back in the classroom, Mrs. Gibbs took up the book she was reading to them. She read a chapter of the book every day after lunch, and today Lucy used this time to do a little more hard thinking. If she and Joey thought Mrs. Gibbs was mean but Sheryl didn't, then who was right? Lucy remembered how Sheryl had turned to look at her that day, the day Mrs. Gibbs dragged Lucy's arm up in the air. Surely she remembered! But she said that she didn't remember. Now that she thought about it, Mrs. Gibbs did seem to be popular with everyone in the class.

They all do what she wants them to do, thought Lucy. But maybe they're not doing it because they're scared, like Joey and me. Lucy stared straight ahead at the folds of the flag. What do they really think of her? She let her eyes go out of focus, blurring the folds of the flag and opened her mind to the thoughts of her classmates. The medallion was warm in her hand. She waited, opening her mind further, trying to shut out the words of the story that was being read aloud, words that seemed to get louder and louder the harder she tried to concentrate on the other children's thoughts.

But that's it! she thought. That's what they're thinking! The story! All together! Lucy was amazed.

This had never happened when Miss Reedy had read to them. Everyone had listened, but thoughts and images came in and around the story, never, *never* everyone thinking the same thing, just repeating the story over in all twenty-four minds.

Lucy caught a flicker of another thought out of the corner of her mind's eye. Homing in on it she was able to draw in the one thought in the room that was not an echo of the story: "Mean, oh meany, afraid. Not fair, that hand, not fair but afraid of her her her her, afraid . . ."

Joey. Lucy sighed. Little Joey was the only other person in the room who was not caught in Mrs. Gibbs's story spell. That conversation at lunch must have got him all worked up.

Suddenly the dull chorus stopped. Lucy looked up and found Mrs. Gibbs looking directly at her. Lucy quickly shifted her eyes, staring at the coarse weave of the striped material hanging in front of her. The woman began reading again and Lucy went on thinking about Joey.

He's so afraid, she thought. Maybe being scared kept Mrs. Gibbs out of Joey's mind. Whatever it was that protected Joey, she wished she had it because today, when Shelley came for her, she was going to have to try to read Mrs. Gibbs's mind.

Just for a moment Lucy looked up and let her

mind focus on the woman who was sitting so straight at the desk, reading aloud in a clear and precise voice from the open book before her. For an instant Lucy had an impression of cold; a bleak, dark chill. The woman's voice stopped, Lucy shivered, and her mind drew back. The woman's hand turned a page and the clear, modulated voice read on and on.

Lucy clasped the Rellard medallion through her shirt and closed her eyes. It wasn't going to be easy. Thank goodness Shelley would be there to protect her!

But Shelley wasn't there. The last bell rang and Lucy waited the five long minutes for Shelley to appear. But the doorway remained empty and there was no protection for her except the little dough Rellard man.

And Joey!

Looking back, Lucy couldn't really work out why Joey had been told to stay after school. All afternoon he had fidgeted and fussed, dropping pencils, crayons, papers, tripping over nothing on the way to the pencil sharpener, spilling the plant water all over the science table, dropping the net into the aquarium, and letting Jeremy's mice loose. That was when Mrs. Gibbs threw up her hands and ordered him to stay after school.

"Clean out your desk!" she thundered, and Joey disappeared behind the upturned lid of his desk, sniffing as he rummaged around in the mess inside.

Having someone else in the room must have broken Mrs. Gibbs's concentration, because instead of filling Lucy's mind with a blank fog of nothingness, she managed only to make her feel heavy and slow.

While the woman was turned away, scolding Joey for upsetting the wastepaper basket that he had dragged over to his desk, Lucy managed to work her arm up under her sweater. She gratefully clasped the little medallion in her right hand and decided to go on with the plan without Shelley.

Their strategy had been simple enough. Shelley would arrive before Mrs. Gibbs had time to work on Lucy. Then, while Shelley was talking with the teacher, Lucy would try to hear what was in her mind. If she was not thinking about the Power of the Rellard, Lucy would give Shelley a signal. Shelley would then say "Rellard!" and Lucy would catch the woman's thoughts.

But now, without Shelley, the plan would have to be changed. Lucy realized that this moment, while Mrs. Gibbs's attention was focused on poor Joey, was a good time to make her move. She grasped the medallion tightly and pushed her thoughts out, searching.

At first she had to deal with a curtain of irritation concerned with Joey. But beyond that, Lucy could feel the woman's mind opening up. She clasped the Rellard man tighter and felt it warm in her hand.

Tell me, she thought. Tell me! and she closed her eyes.

Before her there opened a cold and cruel space, a space that stretched away into darkness on all sides. Lucy's first reaction was that there was nothing there—cold, bare, nothing. But gradually, as she forced her mind on, she came to see that the world of Mrs. Gibbs's thoughts was full—very full. But all was frozen to nothingness by an icy control.

Lucy felt her own mind go cold and bleak, but she pressed on.

The Power of the Rellard, she thought, willing that thought to the woman. The Power of the Rellard!

Deep within Mrs. Gibbs's mind there stirred a great force, a ferocious will.

"Mine," this force murmured. "Mine!" Lucy could feel the tremendous desire the woman had to make the Power of the Rellard her own. "Mine! Mine!" now thundered in the woman's mind, her will unfolding and growing like an evil flower.

Lucy was afraid, but the warmth of the medallion in her hand gave her courage. She threw out one last thought. She pictured Mrs. Gibbs with the Power of the Rellard her own, as her will desired, and thrust that into the dark, cold world of the woman's mind.

"What?" Lucy asked. "What will you do with the Power?"

The answer froze her to her seat in a cruel paralysis of despair. Even the warmth of the medallion faded beneath her hand.

"No," Lucy whimpered. "No, no."

"But yes!" shouted the will of the woman's mind and opened for Lucy a vision of total control—a frozen waste of will turned in on itself, gripped in a deathly chill of power.

Lucy retreated, drawing her bruised thoughts after her. "No!" she whispered, and forced her eyes open.

"Yes! Yes!" screamed Mrs. Gibbs, standing over a cowering, white-faced Joey. "Yes! Yes! You will obey me!" and she raised her arm, the fingers of her hand folded down over the palm.

"Yes!" she screamed, and louder again, "Yes! Yes!"

The windows reflected the figure of the woman against the darkening sky beyond—the light caught on the upraised arm, the strangely folded hand.

"Enough!" screamed the woman. "Enough!" and

she raised the arm higher, fingers trembling over the palm.

Suddenly, Lucy knew that this was the "raised hand" in Rowan's message. And somehow, she also knew that once those fingers—now folded down over the palm—once those fingers were raised, a dreadful power would be unleashed. The palm, the dreadful hidden palm, was directed at Joey, pitiful little Joey.

"No!" Lucy sprang up, the heavy lethargy falling from her like a cloak. She pulled hard on the medallion and the shoelace holding it around her neck parted.

"No! Back, go back!" she shouted and held the little dough medallion high in her twisted hand, pointing it at the woman. The little figure began to glow; Lucy could feel it, see its golden aura spread out from her hand.

But the woman was not to be stopped.

"Mine!" she thundered. "My will, it is to be mine!" She turned the covered palm of her upraised hand toward the little Rellard man. With a scream of rage, she thrust the hand forward and lifted the fingers. From the palm of her upraised hand a dreadful beam of cold fury leaped out toward Lucy, knocking her back against the flag, blasting her with a deathly chill that stopped the breath in her throat, freezing her body, her upraised hand. With her last drop of strength, Lucy threw the medallion directly into that cold fury.

Shelley wrenched open the main door and paused, heart thumping. Ahead of her stretched the hallway, dark except for the slice of yellow that fell from the open door of a classroom. Lucy's classroom!

Shelley was already running when the terrible "Mine!" rang out, and she forced her legs to go faster, faster toward the open door.

The sudden brilliance pouring from the room blinded her and she raised her arm, spreading her fingers against the fierce explosion of light.

"Lucy," she screamed. "Lucy!"

But she was too late. The cold beam had knocked Lucy back, crumpling her against the flag. Shelley screamed again and threw herself into the brilliant light as the glowing medallion arched slowly through the air, turning end over end, the dirty old shoelace trailing gracefully behind. Shelley spread her arms and followed the medallion's slow arc, but before she could catch it, could stop its slow fall, it struck the outstretched palm of the dark woman.

Suddenly the medallion was gone and in its place towered a glowing figure, arm upraised. From its shoulders arched two wings, and white horns circled up from its brow.

"Rowan!" gasped Shelley and fell back.

The giant winged man grasped the upraised arm of the woman, who seemed to be clothed in a swirling darkness, and threw her down. She gave a terrible scream as she fell and her upraised arm twisted beneath her.

Rowan stood looking down at the dark figure at his feet and then he turned to Shelley. He smiled and held out his left hand. Shelley could see something glowing there. She stood up slowly as the tall winged figure approached and she, too, stretched out her hand. Rowan placed the glowing object in the palm of her hand and disappeared.

Lucy opened her eyes. Someone was groaning. She fought her way out of the enveloping folds of the flag and looked around in astonishment.

Mrs. Gibbs lay moaning on the floor, her right arm folded at an impossible angle beneath her body. Joey was cowering beneath his desk and the upset wastepaper basket rolled gently back and forth. Bits of the little dough medallion were spread over the floor, and Shelley stood like a statue, gazing at something in the palm of her hand.

"I want to go home," whimpered Joey.

FIFTEEN

The Magic of the Wand

"What happened then?" Georgie's cheeks were pink with excitement. The three of them were doing the dishes after dinner that night.

Lucy shrugged. "Mr. Nelson came in and told us to go home. I guess he stayed to help Mrs. Gibbs."

"We had to walk Joey home." Shelley stacked the plates carefully.

"Just think! You really saw Rowan!" Georgie's glasses gleamed in the light. "Tell me again what he looked like."

"He has blue wings, just like Lucy said. And the horns." Shelley started to sort the knives from the forks and spoons.

"I wish I hadn't been all tangled up in the flag," grumbled Lucy.

"Did Joey see him?" Georgie asked.

"No, apparently not." Shelley's hands moved calmly and deliberately. "I asked him. He said Mrs. Gibbs tripped over the wastepaper basket." She held a spoon up and inspected it closely. "Here, you'd better do this one again," she said, handing the spoon to Georgie.

Georgie held the spoon under the tap for a moment and handed it to Lucy, who began to rub it on her tea towel.

"I did the *speriment*, just like we planned," said Lucy.

"You did? Good girl!" Georgie gave the dishcloth a final flourish. "Let's go up to my room and talk about it there!"

Later, they sat huddled in a circle on the floor of Georgie's room, wrapped against the cold in blankets and quilts and watched over by the cross-eyed owl.

"Now then," Georgie said, "what did you see when you read Mrs. Gibbs's mind?"

"Cold. Freezing cold."

"Cold? Is that all?" Georgie was disappointed.

Lucy squeezed her eyes shut and pulled the old blanket closer around her shoulders. "There was lots of stuff there. People and machines and things. But they were all cold." She shivered. "It was awful!"

"What does she want the Power of the Rellard for?" Shelley leaned forward. "Were you able to see that?"

"Cold, that's it." Lucy opened her eyes. "That's what she wants it for. To freeze everything."

Georgie frowned. "Weird! Everything frozen like that. Were the people dead?"

Lucy shut her eyes again, the better to visualize what she had seen in the brief moment. "It was all cold but all alive still. Only Mrs. Gibbs could move them," she said.

"Move them?"

"Yes. The people and the machines and things. She had the power over them."

"Ah." Shelley leaned back. "That's why she wants the Power of the Rellard. For control."

Lucy nodded. "That's it. That's the word. Like when she read the story and everybody's mind read the story, too."

"Story? What story?"

Lucy explained about the whole class thinking the story as Mrs. Gibbs read it.

"She was really dangerous!" Georgie said. "And you got rid of her! Good for you, Luce!"

"I don't think she's finished." Shelley's calm voice broke in on Georgie's excited congratulations.

"Why? Why not?" Both Lucy and Georgie challenged her.

"Because of this." Shelley held out her hand. In the palm lay a bright silver coin.

As Georgie and Lucy inspected the coin, Shelley explained how Rowan had stepped forward and laid it in her palm.

"And then he just disappeared and Lucy unwound herself out of the flag," she finished.

"Strange. It's really a strange coin." Georgie had dug a magnifying glass out of the bottom drawer of his desk and was peering closely at the coin. "It has an engraving on it. Here, on this side, it looks like a flower, a stiff-looking lily, or something. What do you think it is?" He handed the coin to Lucy.

"It's for spending," she stated, weighing the coin in her hand. "It's for buying something."

"But what?" Georgie absently rubbed the glass on the blanket. "If you tried to spend it anywhere, no one would take it. It's not legal tender!"

"Look in the comic book," commanded Shelley, and Georgie opened the Rellard comic to the last pages.

"Yup," he chortled. "It's all here—the battle with Mrs. Gibbs, throwing the medallion—hey! Wait a minute!" He carefully tore a coupon from the comic book. "This wasn't here before."

"What's it for?" asked Lucy.

"Do magic tricks! Surprise your friends and amaze your family!" Georgie read. "It's for a wand, a magic wand. It's a coupon for sending for the magic wand."

"How much is it?" asked Shelley.

"Let me see." Georgie mumbled to himself as he read, "Expandable . . . while supplies last . . . name and address . . . ah, here it is. Twelve dollars and ninety-eight cents." He looked up. "Heck! Twelve dollars, almost thirteen dollars. Where are we going to get that much money?"

Shelley held up the coin. "Right here. Just you wait and see."

The next day Georgie took over looking after Lucy and Shelley hurried through the cold to the little jewelery shop down at the end of Taft Street. She had never been in the shop before, but the owner, Mr. Andaclus, was a familiar sight. He always wore his little jeweler's glass fastened to the frame of his spectacles.

Shelley had seen old coins for sale in his dusty window as she walked past on the way to her weekly piano lesson. She clutched the silver coin inside her glove and pushed the door of the shop open. It was dark inside, the glass cases dusty and shadowy.

"Hello?" she called and jumped as a figure loomed out of the dimness. For one horrible moment she thought it was a monster with three eyes. But it was only Mr. Andaclus, with his shining glasses and the jeweler's lens tipped to the side.

"Yes?" He smiled down at her. She drew the silver coin from her glove and placed it on the soft velvet pad on the counter. It shone brightly in the dim shop, the flower pushing roundly up from the silver background.

"Ah," he breathed and swiveled the third glass down. He squinted through it for a long moment, turning the coin several times. At last he straightened and looked at Shelley. His eyebrows lifted in question.

"How much?" Shelley asked.

"You want to sell?"

Shelley nodded.

"Hm-m-m-m-m." Mr. Andaclus retreated to the darkness at the back of the shop and returned with a battered book. Shelley wriggled her cold toes inside her boots and waited patiently as the old man ran his finger up and down the columns of print, whistling softly to himself. Finally his finger stopped.

"Ah!" he said. "Yes," he continued, and picked up the coin in his long fingers. He turned it to look at the flower, then at the reverse side, then back again to the flower.

Then he weighed the coin on a little set of scales, carefully transfering the weights from their round holes in the wooden base to the brass dish on one end of the balancing arm.

Shelley could feel impatience rising in her chest, but she took a deep breath and forced herself to wait silently. This was her message from Rowan and she didn't want to spoil it.

At last Mr. Andaclus replaced the coin in the center of the red velvet pad and spoke.

"Fourteen dollars."

Shelley blinked. Fourteen dollars! Not twelve dollars and ninety-eight cents. She felt cheated.

Mr. Andaclus leaned over the counter. "I added a bit on," he said, "to encourage you."

Shelley could only look at him.

"Yes," he went on, "it's good to see young people interested in coins and collecting. I can sell you some coins, too." He walked to the old cash register, which was crouching in its dusty golden curlicues on the end of the counter. It gave a wheezy ping as he pressed a key and the drawer begrudgingly slid out halfway. Mr. Andaclus gave it a solid yank and fished around in the drawer.

"Here you are," he said as he handed the money

to Shelley. "Fourteen dollars."

"How much did you encourage me?" Shelley asked, folding the notes over and sliding them into her mitten.

"Eh?"

"The coin, what is its real price?"

"Oh." He laughed and riffled the pages of the coin catalogue. "I didn't give you too much more. It's listed at twelve ninety-eight here, but this is an old catalogue and probably . . ." He looked up in astonishment as the door slammed behind the running girl.

"So it was for spending," said Lucy.

"Yes, it was. And the difference between its real price and the price Mr. Andaclus gave me paid for the money order, the envelope, and the stamp!" Shelley grinned triumphantly. She had sent the coupon and money order off that afternoon and the three of them were discussing how long it would take for the wand to arrive.

"What will we use it for when it does come?" Lucy hugged her knees. "That mean old Mrs. Gibbs is gone!"

"Who's your teacher now?"

"Mr. Traveller. He's quiet and smiley." Lucy looked thoughtful. "I couldn't look into his mind but he *feels* okay. And he let me sit back in my old place. No more flag in front of me!" She laughed.

"I wonder," murmured Georgie, "if Mrs. Gibbs is finished with us yet? We should still be careful."

"We know it's something to do with cold," Shelley agreed. "You're right, Georgie, we'll have to watch out and be ready. And speaking of watching out, how was Mr. Boaz today?"

Georgie smiled crookedly. "The same, I guess. I don't know. I'm not in his class anymore. He won't let me."

"What?" Lucy and Shelley were shocked.

"Yep. He said I wasn't objective enough. He didn't like any of the plans I drew up over the holidays." Georgie couldn't hide his disappointment. "I'm in Mr. Neilson's class now."

"Oh, poor Georgie," soothed Lucy.

"No, no, I'll be okay." Georgie spoke quickly. "Don't worry about me. But what about you, Shelley, you and Suzanne?"

Shelley flushed. "She's not speaking to me. She won't even *look* at me!"

"Oh, Shelley, how mean!" Lucy was indignant. "Some friend!"

Shelley shrugged. "Yes, some friend, all right." She hugged her knees and frowned thoughtfully. "But you know, she taught me a lot about *being* a friend. It wasn't all bad."

" 'Course not! You're a terrific friend," Lucy stated loyally. Shelley grinned and pushed Lucy over in a heap. Her stockinged feet stuck out of the quilt, wriggling wildly.

This broke the discussion down into a pushing and shoving match, which deteriorated further when Georgie resorted to swatting at Shelley with a pillow. Their mother yelled up the stairs and Dad came up, stamping loudly. The melee ceased and the three children began to tidy up the mess in Georgie's room.

"Anyway," Georgie said as he replaced the owl on the top shelf, "I'm sure Rowan will tell us what to use the wand for when it comes."

"No school today," Dad announced at breakfast the next morning. It had begun to snow again in the night and the curtain of swirling white blotted out the daylight. The kitchen light shone eerily down on the table.

"The roads are closed and the school heating system has broken down," he continued. "It was on the news."

"Oh, no," said Georgie. "It's started again."

"Speaking of starting," said Dad, "come and help me shovel out the driveway. Then we'll see if we can get the car started."

"It'll be all right," said Shelley as she stacked the breakfast dishes in the sink for Lucy to wash. "They'll fix up the heating system by tomorrow and the snow will stop. Tomorrow, maybe, or the day after."

But Shelley was wrong. The school did not reopen in two or even three days. The snow continued to fall and so did the temperature. The electricity did not fail, but Georgie and the girls brought in more wood and stacked it in the corner of the kitchen, just in case.

At the end of the first week of the Big Freeze, as Georgie called it, Dad and Mum stopped going to work at the studio. No one came in, all the backlog of work was done, and the car had refused to start. Mum popped mounds of popcorn and they sat around the table playing Monopoly. Dad brought all the camping gear up from the basement again.

"It's a real emergency," Georgie stated. "I wish that wand would get here."

"Rowan will get it here," promised Lucy.

On the second day of the second week the electricity failed. They moved into the living room and began to burn the wood from the Big Tree in the fireplace.

It grew even colder. It was as if the vast Arctic

had opened its gates and poured a deep, chill stream down over them, smothering all life and movement. Huddled around the fire, they listened to the long litany of cold disaster on Georgie's little battery-powered radio. All around them, people were huddled in their homes, nursing meager supplies of fuel. Snow blocked roads and railways and airport runways.

"Will we run out of food and starve?" asked Lucy on the fourth day.

Mother quickly reassured her that there was plenty of food, that if they ran out, Dad and Georgie could push through the snowdrifts to the grocery store.

"But what if they aren't open, like the studio?" asked Lucy.

"Don't worry," said Mother. "We'll be fine. This cold can't last forever."

"That's just the trouble," muttered Georgie to Shelley. "If Mrs. Gibbs has her way, it can."

"I wish that wand would hurry up and get here," whispered Shelley.

On the last day of the second week of the Big Freeze, a long brown parcel was thrust through the mail flap. It was addressed to Lucy.

"I put your name on the coupon," explained Shelley. "It was my money but I decided you would be the one to use the wand." The three of them took the parcel to Georgie's room and huddled close around Lucy as she slid the brown paper away to reveal a peacock-blue box embossed with gold lettering.

"Rowan Magic Works," Lucy read.

"Hurry up. Open it!" Georgie's teeth were chattering with the cold and excitement. "Don't be so slow, Lucy!"

Lucy lifted the lid of the box and revealed a nest of blue velvet in which lay a shiny black wand. It twinkled up at them like an old friend.

"Go on, go on! Pick it up!" urged Georgie, breathing little puffs of white in the frigid air of the room.

Slowly Lucy lifted the wand from its velvet nest. It was not very long, but the gradual tapering from one end to the other made it appear longer. Around the larger end there was a golden band with a little lily embossed in it. Lucy turned the wand in her hands and ran her finger over the little flower. She pressed gently and they all jumped in surprise as the wand snapped out to twice its original length.

"Hey! That's really something!" Georgie was delighted.

"How do I make it go back?" Lucy held the wand before her like a sword.

"Press the flower again," advised Shelley, and

sure enough, the wand obediently slid back into itself again.

They tried it out in turn, each swishing the wand in and out, until Georgie brought them back to reality.

"What do we do now?" he asked.

"The comic," answered Shelley, pointing the wand like a baton at Georgie's desk. Georgie shuffled through the papers there, drew out the magazine, and settled down to read.

"It's getting thicker and thicker," he observed, as he leafed through the comic. "Here we are. Let me see . . . the cold, yes . . . everywhere, it is . . . ocean freezing . . . See!" He turned the book to show them.

Shelley shook her head. "You know we can't see it, Georgie. Tell us what it shows us doing with the wand."

"Forgot." Georgie dived into the comic again. "Well, it shows us going up to the top of Hawker Rock with the wand. Wait a minute. . . . Yep, we have to go up there."

"How?" demanded Shelley.

"Sled."

"We don't have a sled!" Lucy protested.

"Wait!" said Georgie. "There's four of us. You,

me, Luce, and someone bigger pulling Lucy on the
sled. I can't see who it is because the face is all covered up with a scarf, the bottom part, anyway."

"A man?" Shelley frowned.

"What color coat?" asked Lucy.

"Red," Georgie answered. "With a red-and-
white-striped scarf."

"Carrie!" Lucy shouted. "Come on!"

"Hawker Rock!" Carrie was aghast. "Hike all the
way up to the Rock now? In this snow?" They were
standing just inside the front door of the Carney
house, knee-deep in a jumble of boots and coats.

"With a sled. Your sled. We don't have one."

Carrie just went on staring.

"Please, Carrie." Lucy put her mittened hand on
the older girl's arm. "It's important. You know."

"The tree thing?" Carrie asked.

Lucy nodded.

Carrie stamped into heavy boots, shrugged into a
bright red coat, and wound herself into a long red-
and-white-striped scarf.

"Back in a while," she yelled over her shoulder
and led the way around the house to the garage. The
long sled that she lifted down from its hook up in
the rafters looked a bit rickety but its runners whispered smoothly along behind them over the snow.

The deep snow and the cold pulled at them, dragging at their boots, stinging tears from their eyes. Carrie plodded steadily on, breaking a trail for Georgie and Shelley to pull the sled with Lucy on it smoothly up the hill. They were exhausted by the time they reached the top of Hawker Rock; they stood leaning on one another, gasping for breath, knees trembling with the effort.

Georgie was the first to recover.

"Look," he said.

Spread out before them was a completely white landscape beneath a dull gray sky. The corner of a roof, the branch of a tree, a partly cleared path, a chimney—these few details broke into the total white. Nothing moved except the spirals of smoke from the chimneys.

"Looks like more snow." Carrie's voice was muffled by her scarf. She pointed off to the west, where the gray sky bulged earthward, showing a dark edge. "Just what we need."

Lucy climbed off the sled and stood between her brother and sister.

"Should I do it now?" she asked.

"What about . . . ?" Georgie jerked his head at Carrie, who was staring morosely at the gathering gloom to the west.

"She's okay," and Lucy reached under her heavy

jacket and pulled out the wand. She held it in her teeth while she pulled off her mitten and stuffed it in her pocket. Then she carefully pressed the golden lily and the wand sprang to its full length.

Carrie eyed the wand and shrugged. "I'll just be down the hill a bit," she said, and moved back down the trail with the sled.

"She's guarding," explained Lucy. "Now, what will I do?"

"Just do what feels natural," advised Shelley.

Lucy took the wand in her right hand and held it out straight over the town and river below. Then, slowly at first, but gradually quickening, she started to move the wand. The tip began to glow, and as it circled and swooped it left a trail of light in the air; a trail of signs and symbols that grew and grew.

Georgie recognized some of the symbols. He had seen them in a physics book that Mr. Boaz had lent him. But he could not make sense of the whole cloud of light that floated in the still cold air before them.

Shelley squinted at the trailings of light and saw flowers—strange, exotic blooms that went from bud to blossom to bud again, and mingled together in an intricate garland.

Lucy bit her lower lip and continued moving the wand, adding to the figures of light that rose and floated out over the valley below, dispersing and moving away in all directions.

At last she lowered the wand, pressed the golden lily to retract it, and stood with her brother and sister watching the cloud of light move away from them.

"What do you think?" she finally asked.

"Don't know." Georgie lifted his head and sniffed the air. "Something! Something's different!"

Shelley bent and picked up a gloveful of snow. "Look!"

The snow, which had been so cold and dry that it looked like flakes of soap, was changing. It was becoming softer, wetter. Before their eyes, it plumped up in a moist snowy mound on Shelley's mitten. She brought the other hand down on it and squeezed the snow into a round, hard ball.

"Yippee!" she yelled and threw the snowball into the air. "You've done it, Lucy! You've broken the cold!"

And they all three began to jump up and down, yelling and shouting with relief. Carrie came tramping up from her lookout and Georgie grabbed her arm.

"Look!" he yelled. "She did it! *We* did it! We *all* did it!"

Carrie looked out over the valley. She turned to the west, where the dark edge of cloud was lifting. Then she looked to the east and behind them, to the south. She smiled down at Lucy.

"I knew you were special," she said.

Lucy tucked the wand under her jacket.

"Come on. Let's slide back home," she said.

They piled on the sled, gripping each other around the waist, Carrie's long legs on each side, working the creaky crossbar. Down from the Rock they swooped, down the steep slope, across the river bridge, down and down and around the long curve to the flat.

The next day, the news announcer read a list of schools that would be opening again, now that the cold had lifted, and their school was one of them. Plows were gradually shifting the snow and Dad went out and started the car. The refrigerator and lights came on again and Mother went shopping.

"That warm front really saved us," commented Dad. "It looks like we may be finished with the winter." They were eating in the dining room tonight.

Lucy smiled at Shelley and Georgie.

SIXTEEN

Taking Precautions

The next month saw a return to normal. The long cold winter gradually loosened its grip. The snow kept on melting, running down the roofs of the houses, freezing at night into long cold swords of ice that sparkled and dripped in the next day's sunshine. The soft snow was perfect for packing and every house sported at least one snowman.

A brisk battle was fought with the Carney boys from the round snow fort that Shelley and Georgie built. Lucy made snowballs until her fingers were blue, but it was worth it. They beat off two frontal attacks and one sneaky infiltration from the rear, finally chasing the Carney boys home. They retired victorious and sat around the kitchen table, swinging their stockinged feet and drinking hot chocolate with floating marshmallows.

Lucy bloomed at school. Mr. Traveller was quiet and Lucy felt safe with him. When Jeremy asked what had happened to Mrs. Gibbs, the answer was that Mrs. Gibbs had fallen and hurt her arm and would not be back. Lucy settled happily to work.

Georgie was happy with his work, too. One day he went into Mr. Boaz's room to collect his plans for his experiments and projects. Mr. Boaz had sent an announcement around, asking all the special-class students to pick up their work. It was stacked neatly on a side table and Georgie hummed to himself as he sorted through the papers.

When he turned to go, Mr. Boaz was barring the way.

"I hope you're satisfied!" he rasped.

Georgie blinked.

"Don't stand there looking stupid!"

Georgie clutched his papers to his chest, suddenly afraid. "I'm sorry, sir," he mumbled and tried to sidle around the man to the door.

"It's not over, you know!" Mr. Boaz towered over the boy, shouting. "Tell that crippled sister of yours it's not over!"

Georgie fled.

Later, when he thought about it, he decided not to say anything to Lucy.

It will just worry her! he protested to himself. And it *is* over. The cold is gone. He's just angry because *they* lost!

The next week, Mr. Boaz was not at school. He would not be returning, they said. Georgie was relieved that he would not have to face the man again.

Shelley found, to her surprise, that it was she and not Suzanne who now seemed to collect friends. She smiled and everyone smiled back.

"Who are all these people that keep tying up the telephone?" demanded Dad.

"They're my friends!" said Shelley. "They want to talk to me."

"You see them all day at school! What else can you find to say after school? Why can't it wait until the next day? It's like a siege!"

"Daddy!" protested Shelley and then saw that he was teasing her.

"Okay, Shell, but no calls after nine o'clock," and Dad snapped the newspaper up in front of his face.

The account books were evidently behaving. Mum spent less time worrying at the lines of figures and was even talking of hiring some part-time help at the studio, so that she could come home earlier.

Best of all, Dad's heart trouble was easing. The gray tone was leaving the skin around his eyes and his old bounce and sparkle were returning. He punched Georgie's stomach and teased Shelley and Lucy.

"Spring is in the air." Mum laughed.

The news commentators spoke of the possibility of heavy floods to come, when the last of the snow melted.

"Will it flood here?" Lucy looked worried.

"The dams will save us," and Georgie immediately swung into an explanation of flood control and how the dams that barred the flow of their river would ease the high water gradually down its course. He used the serving dishes, the salt and pepper shakers, Shelley's clean knife, and Lucy's well-licked spoon to outline the flood-control program on the dinner table.

"Also," he finished, "as the melting goes on gradually, the danger of flooding lessens. A lot of the water sinks into the ground."

"You explained that very well, Georgie." Dad smiled, and Georgie's face flushed with pleasure.

Just as Georgie had predicted, the gradual warming kept the melting of the snow to a reasonable pace and talk of floods lessened.

* * *

A couple of weeks later, Dad and Mum sat at the dinner table, clearly brimming with excitement.

"Remember the little Saunders girl?"

"Dad, how could we forget her?"

"Yeah, Bitsy the Brat!"

"The worst sitting you ever had, you said," commented Shelley.

"She was, and is!" Dad took a bite and began to chew, eyes twinkling.

"Well?" prodded Georgie.

Dad shook his head, pointing to his chewing mouth.

"Tell us, Daddy," pleaded Lucy.

"Hurry up! Swallow!"

Mum was laughing.

"Tell us! Tell us!" Even the usually calm Shelley was excited and leaned forward to touch her father's hand.

Dad gave an enormous swallow. "Okay! Okay!" He spread his hands wide. "The first half of my announcement concerns Bitsy Saunders, an obnoxious little child who was unable to sit still long enough for me to focus the camera and whose disposition is soured to the point where I'm sure she'll never smile —*that* child has won for me the first prize in the Professional Photographers' Award!"

For a moment there was a stunned silence and

then they all three spoke at once. When comparative calm was once again established, Dad went on to the second half of his announcement.

"I'm going up to the city for the Award dinner. I'd like to accept the prize personally. *And,*" here he beamed down the table at Mum, "your mother's coming with me. We're going to give ourselves a little holiday in the big city."

A small ping of warning sounded in Lucy's mind.

"You're going away?" she asked.

"Just for five days." Mum was smiling.

Georgie looked at Lucy and felt a tiny curl of fear in the pit of his stomach. "Who . . ." He had to clear his throat. "Who will look after us?"

"Not Mrs. Dodds, please." Shelley hunched her shoulders.

"We've always had Mrs. Dodds to babysit," Dad said. "She's a fine . . ."

"Carrie!" interrupted Lucy. "Carrie could do it!"

"Yes. Carrie is very responsible," agreed Shelley. She too was feeling a bit apprehensive about this trip her parents were taking.

"And you don't get a sore throat, yelling at her," muttered Georgie.

"Well, I'll talk to Mrs. Carney about it," agreed Mum. "Now, who wants dessert?"

* * *

"Where did you get that great owl?" Carrie asked. She had moved in and was being escorted by the three children to their parents' room, where she would be sleeping. She had stopped to peer through the open door of Georgie's room.

Georgie offered to lend Carrie the owl for the time she was with them. The owl seemed to look best on the dressing table, his crooked wings reflected in the mirror.

"Thank you, Georgie," Carrie said. "I'll feel safer with owl on guard."

"Safer?" Shelley stroked the owl's wing. "Why safer?"

Carrie began to unpack her bag.

"Don't know." She inspected a slipper. "Just safer. To tell you the truth," she turned to face them, slipper in hand, "I've been feeling a bit . . . funny."

Georgie leaned on the bed. "What do you mean, funny? Everything's okay now."

"After the wand business I was fine." Carrie nodded. "But here lately . . . I don't know." She drew the other slipper from the bag and looked at it. Taking a deep breath, she went on, "I just have this funny feeling that something bad is going to happen. I feel it just here!" and she smacked her midriff with the slipper. She looked at Lucy.

"But it's all over, isn't it? Lucy asked Georgie.

Georgie shrugged. "There aren't any more pages in the comic," he said. "I checked this morning." He clapped his hands together. "I'm sure there's nothing to worry about!"

"You're hiding something!" accused Shelley.

"I'm not." Georgie turned to go.

"Yes, you are! I can tell!" Shelley insisted. "You come back here, Georgie, and tell us the truth!"

Georgie turned at the door, face sober.

"Tell us!"

"Look, it was just a passing remark." Georgie smacked his palm on the door frame.

"Who said it?"

Georgie examined the paint on the door frame. "Mr. Boaz."

"Mr. Boaz!" Shelley threw out her arms. *"You* know what he is! He's one of *them*. Anything he says is important!"

"Who's them?" asked Carrie.

"The people that froze everything. The bad ones," explained Lucy.

Carrie's hands gripped the slipper tightly.

"What did he say?" Shelley's voice was low and demanding.

Georgie began picking at the paint with his thumbnail. "He said that it wasn't over, yet."

"That's all? That's it?"

Georgie continued picking. He gave a little shake of his head.

"He said something about me, didn't he, Georgie?" Lucy went to stand in front of her brother.

Georgie nodded.

"Go on, tell us. It won't hurt me." Lucy spoke softly. "Go on, Georgie. Tell us."

"He said." Georgie stopped, looked at Lucy and then went on quickly. "He said, 'tell that crippled sister of yours, it's not over yet.' And before that, he said he hoped we were satisfied!"

Lucy flinched slightly at the word crippled. A wrinkle of worry grew between her eyebrows.

"Not over yet," she whispered. She turned to face Carrie and Shelley.

"We'll have to watch out, be really careful," she warned. "They must want the Power really bad. They still might win!" Her eyes grew large and dark. "I've been feeling a bit funny here, too," and she patted the front of her shirt.

The four of them stood frozen in an instant of apprehension. Then Carrie broke the spell.

"See if a couple of these don't help." She smiled, and hauled a bag of her special chocolate chip cookies from a corner of her suitcase.

They all laughed then, but later, before they went

to bed that night, Carrie confided to Shelley that she was more worried than before.

"I keep looking around for someone!" she explained. "It's like somebody is sneaking up on me!"

The four of them checked all the windows and doors together and left the kitchen light on all night.

The next day their mother telephoned to say that she and Dad were having a great time and what about them?

"We're fine, just fine," Shelley assured her mother and handed the phone over to Carrie, who reported that there was plenty of food, no problems, yes, everything was just fine.

"Go on," prompted Georgie. "Ask her."

Getting Mum to say yes to a Saturday afternoon at the movies was an ordeal requiring vast reserves of persuasion, and Georgie and Shelley were hoping to throw their mother off guard by getting Carrie to ask for them.

"Your Mum doesn't like movies much, does she?" Carrie commented after she hung up the receiver.

"Yes or no?" It was a space adventure and Georgie loved those.

"Yes, but don't you do that to me again, set me up like that!"

"Mum thinks that movies are like sleeping pills.

They put your mind to sleep! She's always saying that." Shelley began to clear the table.

"I know, I know. I just had five minutes of it." Carrie picked up her plate.

"I don't want to go," said Lucy.

"Some science fiction movies are classics," said Georgie. "They're almost educational."

"I'll stay home," said Lucy.

"Educational!" snorted Carrie.

"I don't like space ships and all those robots," said Lucy.

"Come on, Lucy," called Shelley. "It's your turn to wipe."

"I'll be okay all by myself," said Lucy.

"You won't be by yourself," said Shelley. "Carrie's going, too, and we can all sit together."

"No, here at home. I'll be okay."

"Lucy, what *are* you talking about? We're going to the movie. Mother said we could."

Lucy threw down her tea towel. "You *never* listen to me! I've been telling you and telling you."

"Telling what?" Lucy had everyone's attention now.

"I do not want to go to the movie. I will stay here at home alone and I will be okay. There!" Lucy picked up the tea towel and began on a plate.

"But you can't," said Carrie. "I'm supposed to be

looking after you. All three of you. I can't leave you here alone."

"She's right, you know," said Georgie. "Come on, Luce. Come to the movie with us."

"You don't want to stay home alone," said Shelley.

"You *can't* stay home alone," Carrie stated. "If you don't go, *we* don't go."

"Lucy!" Shelley stood, hands on hips.

"You just never listen." Lucy started on another plate. "I told you and told you that I don't like space movies."

"Could she stay at your place? Would your mother mind?" Georgie asked Carrie.

"Of course not! Mum won't even notice one more." Carrie laughed. "I'll go and tell her."

"Will you do that?" asked Shelley. "Will you go over to the Carneys' place while we go to the movie?"

"Yes." Lucy nodded. "I can keep an eye on things from over there."

Shelley looked thoughtful. "Things? What things?"

"Oh, just all our things. You know," replied Lucy.

"I think I'll go and clean up my room," said Georgie.

Georgie surveyed his unmade bed and then leaned

over to draw the bedspread up and over the rumpled blankets. He spent quite some time patting out the larger lumps. He stood by the bed, thinking, and then disarranged it entirely as he hunted out the Rellard comic from under the mattress. The colorful magazine was thicker and Georgie sat down to read. He muttered to himself as he flipped over the pages, running his fingers through his hair and shoving his glasses up on his nose.

"Nothing here . . . should be safe," he muttered. He closed the book and began to put it away under the mattress again. Then he stopped. "No," he said aloud, and turned to his cupboard.

Fifteen minutes later, Georgie had completely waterproofed the comic. It was swathed in plastic, weighted down with a flat stone and sealed with waterproof tape.

"That ought to do it," he said. He had to wait until Shelley finished washing her hair in the bathroom before he could go in and drop the bag into the cistern of the toilet. The plastic parcel sank and lay below the ballcock apparatus.

"Safe," Georgie muttered.

Lucy's remark about keeping an eye on things had sent Shelley straight to the little chest where she kept the Rellard notebook. The chest sat in plain view on top of the chest of drawers.

"Anybody could find it," she thought, and went in search of a strong plastic bag. She sealed the Rellard notebook into the bag with tape, smoothing out all the trapped air until she had a neat, flat parcel.

Then Shelley began an erratic wandering through the house, stopping to consider, shaking her head, going on, coming back, mumbling to herself—pacing out her indecision. Her cheeks grew pink with frustration.

Finally she stopped, the package hugged to her chest, and stood stock-still for a long moment. Her eyes were squeezed shut and she seemed to stop breathing.

"Of course!" Her eyes shot open and she marched purposefully out to the sunroom, which was a green blaze of sunshine, her mother's houseplants lined up three deep on the window ledges and specially built glass shelves.

In one corner, rearing up in solitary grandeur, was a gigantic fern. Its fronds reached the floor. Shelley parted the foliage and dug into the damp soil below. She dug carefully, going down next to the side of the earthenware pot in which the plant grew. Finally she was able to shove the plastic-encased notebook into the pot and pat it down under a layer of soil. The leftover dirt she portioned out to the other potted plants.

"Safe." She smiled, and went to wash her hair.

Meanwhile Lucy had finished wiping the dishes and slowly climbed the stairs to her room. There she pulled the black wand from under her pillow. She polished it on a corner of the sheet and pressed the little flower on the gold ring. The wand whispered sleekly in and out. She waved it in the air one last time, collapsed it, and hid it in her sleeve. With one arm stuck straight down her side, she made her way to the basement and the tool room.

Junk room, their mother always called it. It did have some tools in it, along with piles of papers, boxes, broken furniture, hoses, croquet sets, and much more. Lucy marched straight to the far wall and drew the wand from her sleeve. Long nails protruding from the wall formed brackets on which were stored a motley assortment of pipes, tubes, poles, and rings of wire. Lucy carefully laid the wand between two rusty nails that already supported some old tubing. For a moment the shiny black wand glowed brightly, standing out against its tawdry neighbors. Then it faded and seemed to grow old, dusty, and tarnished—blending in completely.

"Stay safe," whispered Lucy, and climbed the steps to the kitchen.

SEVENTEEN

Attack of the Fire Beasts

The trouble with the Carneys, thought Lucy, is that they don't pay attention.

Lucy had been dropped off at the Carney house with a brisk good-bye from the other three as they hurried off to their movie. Lucy was immediately included in a lively game that involved the shaking and throwing of dice and the moving of little plastic rabbits around a board. No one could explain the rules to her and everyone accused everyone else of cheating, so Lucy was afraid of cheating accidentally and let the youngest Carney take her turn. She gradually moved away from the table and sidled into the living room.

The television set was going full blast with the cat

fast asleep on top of it. Mr. Carney was fast asleep on the sofa. Lucy felt uncomfortable watching television with Mr. Carney there, asleep, so she dodged around the fight that had broken out between the owner of the blue bunny and the owner of the red bunny and peeped into the kitchen. Mrs. Carney was talking on the telephone and stirring something in a pot on the stove.

This was when Lucy had her thought about not paying attention, because it seemed to her that she was invisible to the Carneys. However, right at that lonely moment, she was caught up in a raucous game of hide-and-seek and she didn't have time to stop and think again until she was hiding in Carrie's bedroom.

She knew that it was Carrie's room because it was so neat and it had a window that faced the empty piece of sky left when the Big Tree fell.

"This is where she was when she saw me do the Trial of the Tree," thought Lucy. She rested her chin on folded arms and considered, from this new perspective, the familiar landscape beyond the window. There was the stump of the Big Tree, the shed, the woodpile, her house—the house!

Lucy sat up straight, heart beating in quick panic. The house! Something was wrong with the house!

What? What was it?

Lucy sprang up and pressed her face against the window.

There! There again! A quick wink of red!

"Fire!"

Lucy turned and ran—ran down through the Carney boys, past the oblivious Mrs. Carney, ran out the door and across the gardens, ran in panic to her house, where the fire flickered and winked behind the windows.

She could smell smoke as she twisted the knob on the front door.

Locked! Her hands trembled as she scrabbled for the key under the mat. Where *was* it? Gone! Gone to the matinee in Carrie's pocket.

Lucy whimpered in fear and frustration. She turned and raced around the house to the back door but found it locked against her. She stood, sobbing, and then caught a whisper of smoke, a faint whisper curling out from the partly open basement window that no one had noticed.

Without thinking, Lucy wriggled through the window backwards, hanging by her good hand, finally dropping to the floor. The smoke stung her eyes as she stumbled up the cellar stairs to the door at the top. In the kitchen there was more smoke and a crackling from the hall beyond. Spirals of smoke were eddying down the stairs, threading the banisters. An acrid curtain hung over the head of the stairs.

Lucy began to climb.

Halfway up, as the stairs brought her eyes level with the floor above, she saw the fire. Her scalp prickled and she retreated one step, shrinking back against the railing.

It was like no fire she had ever seen! It flared and crackled and spewed spirals of smoke, but even though it raged along the hall, the carpet and walls remained untouched. It was as if a wild beast—a hunting animal—had been fashioned from fire and let loose upstairs in Lucy's house. It was prowling, creeping along the floor, snuffling under the door to Georgie's room, throwing a crackling flare into the girls' room; searching, prying, filling the air with its acrid fury and smoky stench.

Suddenly, the fiery beast seemed to become aware of Lucy and it lashed out with a burning claw.

Lucy shrank back further, terrified. What was she to do?

The fire beast moved purposefully down the hall to the door of Georgie's room. It growled and thundered against the panels, throwing out tendrils of flame to thrust beneath the closed door, twisting the knob, assaulting the keyhole. Finally the doorknob turned, slowly at first, then faster as the flames surged around and over it. With a roar of triumph, the flames thrust and heaved through the now open door.

The book! The comic book! That was what the fiery beast was seeking!

"Get out!" yelled Lucy, stumbling up the stairs. "Get out of here!" she screamed from the door of Georgie's room. The flame beast reared up and roared back at her, showing jagged yellow fangs in a snarl of fire.

Lucy stumbled back against the wall, arm up to protect her face. The beast turned and resumed its fiery search of Georgie's room. But now it was consuming its prey, throwing out flaming bits of paper, which drifted down to smoulder on the rug, melting the plastic airplanes and creeping up the curtains. Heat and smoke billowed out the door, enveloping Lucy.

She sagged against the door of her parents' bedroom, throat raw and eyes blinded by hot tears. She fell back and a rush of cool air told her that she was through the door. There was no flame beast here! She sank to her knees, coughing, wiping the tears on her sleeve.

Outside, the beast moved from Georgie's room

bellowing its frustration, roaring louder and louder. It began to grow, throwing out a tremendous heat.

"No!" sobbed Lucy, as the one fiery beast became two and then three separate flaming creatures. The smallest remained in Georgie's room, turning and twisting amid the smoking remains of Georgie's collection. The second rushed to Shelley and Lucy's room and started another fiery search. The third began to creep toward Lucy, licking out small tongues of fire, creeping on yellow clawed paws of flame, stalking Lucy as any beast stalks its prey.

Lucy shrank back, sobbing, eyes smarting from the heat and smoke. The beast crept closer and closer across the carpet. Lucy retreated, falling back until she felt the hard edge of the dressing table pressing into her back. She could go no further. She raised her arm, hand spread against the flame, and hid her eyes, waiting for the first touch of the fire's bite.

But that bite never came. Lowering her arm, Lucy could see the beast, hesitating a step away from her. It leaped and snarled, but came no nearer. Something was stopping it. Something was keeping it from making its final pounce!

She turned her head slowly, keeping track of the lunging fire out of the corner of her eye. The glassy crossed eyes of Georgie's stuffed owl were practically touching her nose. Her throat closed in a gasp as one eye slowly blinked at her! The owl blinked the other eye and stretched its wings fully, creating a tawny span of wing and feather.

The fiery beast before Lucy shrank and retreated, snarling.

Smiling now, Lucy stretched out her right arm and the great tawny owl settled gently there, gripping with its gnarled claws, wings spread wide. Together they moved against the beast of flame, forcing it out the door, down the hall, against the wall.

With each beat of the owl's wings, the fire shrank and cowered—dodging, turning—consuming itself in its rage to escape.

Lucy and the owl managed to corner the three fire beasts at the end of the hallway. There they made a last stand, leaping and lunging, swept in ever-decreasing circles.

A strange transformation began to take place. The fire ceased to be a creature of heat and light. Its substance began to congeal, becoming plastic, ropy, thick. The heat drained away and, as the owl's wings beat on, the thick, glassy fire became smaller, slower —its energy deadened, its brilliance quenched. It rolled in on itself, slower and slower, until at last there was nothing left but a glassy lump in the corner of the hallway.

Lucy knelt and picked it up. It was very heavy and gave off a dull red glow. The owl folded its wings and resumed its glassy unfocused stare. Lucy returned it to the dressing table in her parents' room and stood considering what to do with the lumpy remains of the fire beast. She decided to put it in the freezer compartment of the refrigerator, and did so. Then she went back to the Carney house, letting herself in quietly through the kitchen. No one had even missed her, although Mrs. Carney remarked on the smudges on her face.

Carrie and her three charges stood and looked at the mess.

"My models! All my model planes! Gone!" Georgic moaned. "And look at my desk!"

They looked. Not one scrap of paper remained whole or unblackened by the flames. The drawers sagged crazily, spilling ashes onto the rug.

"All my notebooks," Georgie cried. "All my papers, my notes! Gone!"

"The comic? The Rellard comic book?" Lucy asked.

Georgie turned and ran to the bathroom. The others followed and watched as he groped in the cistern, water sloshing onto the floor.

"Safe!" He laughed, as his arm emerged with the plastic parcel in his hand. He ripped open the plastic. "Just a bit damp, but safe!"

"The notebook! That's what it wanted in our room!" Shelley dashed off to retrieve the notebook from the fern pot and Lucy hurried down to the basement to where the black wand rested anonymously on the rusty nails.

"These things must be very powerful." Carrie was studying the wand, the comic, and the notebook as they lay on the kitchen table. "Whoever is behind this must want them pretty badly."

"Yes, it's the bad ones, all right," said Georgie. "And I don't think they're finished."

"What do we do with these things now?" Shelley pointed to the table.

"Put them in with the dead fire," said Lucy, and they gathered up the two books and the wand and made a place for them in the icy depths of the freezing compartment. The refrigerator began to hum importantly.

"Now," said Carrie. "Let's get that mess upstairs cleaned up."

* * *

That night the fine weather broke, and it began to rain. Water fell in huge slabs, buffeting the house and wrenching at the trees. The wind rose and added its muscle to the rain.

Lucy sat up in bed. "I'm scared," she whimpered.

"It's just a storm," Shelley said, but she sat up too, and Lucy noticed that her sister flinched when the lightning raged across the sky.

"Are you all right, Georgie?" called Carrie softly.

Although they had worked hard, they hadn't been able to make much headway in cleaning up the mess left by the searching fire beast. So they had decided to sleep in Carrie's room—the three girls in the double bed and Georgie rolled up in a sleeping bag on the floor beside them. The owl stood sentinel on the dressing table.

"Yes. I'm okay," answered Georgie. "I think," he added, as another huge bolt of lightning rampaged across the sky.

"A cup of cocoa would be nice," Shelley suggested, and that was when they discovered that the electricity was off.

Georgie groped around in his room and finally emerged sooty and triumphant, a huge flashlight in his hand.

"Ladies, some light," he announced, and sure

enough, the fire-blackened flashlight responded to the click of its switch and produced a strong yellow beam.

The phone rang. Carrie's mother wanted them to come over to the Carney house but Carrie finally convinced her that they were safe where they were.

"We'll wait the storm out, Mum. It shouldn't be too long," and Carrie hung up.

But the storm showed no sign of weakening, rather it gathered itself in a howling crescendo of fury and crashed about the house. The telephone gave a weak ping. Georgie picked up the receiver and listened a moment, glasses flaring in the light of the torch.

"Dead," he announced.

"Something is happening," said Lucy, hugging her arm. "I can just feel it. Something bad, really bad, is happening."

"Let's check the comic," suggested Georgie, and they followed the yellow beam of his light into the kitchen.

The plastic encasing the notebook and the comic was brittle with frost and a thin layer of ice covered the black wand. Before closing the door of the freezer compartment, Lucy reached far in and lifted out the knobby red glass ball that was the remains of the fire beast. She sat quietly at the kitchen table, cradling the red lump in her lap while Georgie scanned the last few pages of the magazine.

"Well?" prompted Shelley. "What does it say?"

Georgie frowned and turned back a few pages. "It tells about the fire beast. You were really brave, Luce, to tackle that fire like that!"

"I had the owl," said Lucy, gazing down at the lump of glass in her lap.

"Yes," Georgie agreed. "Who would have thought that old owl had magic?"

"Don't go on about the owl." Shelley sternly brought Georgie back to the point. "Is something happening, something to do with the bad ones?"

As if in reply, a stunning blaze of lightning flared through the kitchen windows, followed immediately by an avalanche of thunder. Georgie's glasses blazed white in the lightning and showed round, scared eyes as the thunder tumbled and crashed around the house.

"It doesn't tell about the storm," he said. "It ends with Lucy holding the fire lump."

They all looked at Lucy.

"Yes." She nodded. "Yes."

Slowly she lifted the red glass lump in her two hands and set it carefully on the table.

"It's getting warm," she whispered.

"Oh, Luce!" Shelley's indrawn breath of astonishment spoke for all of them as they sat mesmerized by the now softly glowing glass.

The lump was quite large, about the size of a small pumpkin, and knobby. These knobs showed clearly as the red fire continued to glow, brighter and brighter, washing the faces of the four children in a soft rosy light.

"Inside," said Lucy. "It's inside it."

They all leaned closer and gazed intently into the glowing red mass.

"What is it?" Carrie asked. "I can't tell . . . what is it?" Her voice rose and cracked. Lucy reached out and patted the older girl's arm.

"Looks like the Rock," replied Georgie, peering closer. "Yep. That's Hawker Rock and there," he put a finger on one side of the glowing lump, "there's the town, and that's the river, running around the Rock. Wow! Look at that river!"

Carrie huddled closer to Lucy, who put her arm around the older girl. "It's like a crystal ball," she said, "showing us what is going to happen. Do you think that's what it is, Georgie?"

Georgie shook his head. "A crystal ball, yes, but . . ."

Outside the thunder of the rain grew even louder and the lightning raged. Inside the glowing glass ball, a small fierce flicker of light matched the burst in the sky outside the window.

"It's happening now," whispered Carrie. "Oh, this is weird!"

"Look at that river rise!" Georgie's glasses reflected the miniature turbulence in the glass. "It's flooding!"

Lucy bent closer and touched the knobby lump with her right hand.

"Look," she whispered. "There! There they are!"

On the tiny horizon that stretched beyond Hawker Rock in the glass, there reached down from the black clouds three sinuous tendrils that gradually became stronger, thicker, groping for the ground until at last they touched, sending up small explosions of debris. A tiny barn lifted whole for a moment and then disintegrated in a burst of flying wood.

"No!" protested Carrie.

"Tornadoes," announced Georgie, leaning, fascinated, over the glass. "Real whirlwinds. Twisters!"

"They're coming this way. See!" Shelley pointed.

"Yes. Moving toward the town." Georgie rubbed his forehead. "They'll destroy it. They'll destroy us!"

Inside the red lump a small, lonely farmhouse was blasted by the center funnel. One moment it was there, a faint light glowing through its windows. The next second it had been destroyed, the small light vanished in the wreckage of board and brick.

"That's what will happen to us," whispered Lucy.

"To the whole town!" Georgie's voice was hoarse. "Destroyed! Everybody! Everything! Dogs, people, houses, cars!"

Carrie cried out, "Mum! My mum! And Dad and the boys!"

"Look! There's another one!" Shelley pointed. Behind the first three evil twisting funnels there appeared another, even larger than the three running before it. Outside, a new note was added to the roar of the wind.

"What will we do?" Carrie was shivering.

"They have sent the whirlwinds," said Lucy. "We have to stop them before they get to the town!"

"We haven't got much time." Georgie stood up. "What do we need to do, Lucy?"

Lucy leaned closer to the glowing red glass and gazed intently for a moment.

"We will need the Orb and the Crown."

Georgie groaned. "Lucy, they're buried! Remember? We can't dig them up in this storm!"

"I can see us," Lucy went on, ignoring Georgie. "I can see us on Hawker Rock and I have the Crown, here," she touched her forehead, "and the Orb. And the wand."

"But the tornadoes will get here before we have

time to dig up the Orb and the Crown and get up to Hawker Rock." Shelley's voice trembled slightly.

"I'll stop them for a while." Lucy placed her right hand on the glowing lump of glass and closed her eyes tightly. Her hand grew taut and stiffened with an invisible force, and when she lifted it, the four black funnels stood whirling in place, their forward movement halted.

"We have a little time now"—Lucy's face was pale—"but we must hurry!"

EIGHTEEN

The Towers of Darkness

Shelley opened the Rellard notebook to the map that Georgie had drawn on the day of the bonfire.

"How many steps is it from the corner of the house? The code, Georgie! Read the code!"

"Let me see." Georgie bent low over the map, mumbling to himself. "Twenty-four." He put his finger on the circle that marked the granite rock in the Jacobsen cellar. "I'll go over there and flash my light, in a cross, like this." He demonstrated. "You'll have to pace the twenty-four steps toward the light. Got it?"

Shelley and Carrie nodded. Lucy was still gazing into the glowing remains of the fire beast.

"Come on, Lucy," Carrie urged gently, and they

quickly shrugged into jackets, pulled on boots, and stood for a moment inside the back door, listening to the pounding fury of the storm on the other side. Carrie gripped a shovel and Shelley was carrying a second flashlight that she found under the sink in the kitchen. Lucy stuffed the wand down the front of her jacket and the red glass lump sagged in her pocket.

"Right," said Georgie. "This is it," and he opened the door. The wind immediately whipped it from his hand and smashed it against the side of the house. It also snatched the children and tumbled them into the battering rain.

"Hang on!" Georgie shouted. "Hang on to hands!" he yelled, and the four children gripped hands and staggered across the yard in the direction of the shed.

"It's gone!" Shelley's hand gripped Georgie's even tighter. "It's been blown away!"

The remains of the wooden shed were strewn haphazardly across the yard. In the blazing flashes of lightning and the watery glow of Georgie's torch, the wreckage was plain to see.

Georgie was the first to recover.

"The house! The corner!" he shouted against the blast of the storm. He then pointed to himself and in the direction of the Jacobsen place. Shelley nodded and drew Carrie and Lucy along the side of the house.

"Careful! Be careful, Georgie!" Lucy's words were shredded by the wind, but Georgie caught the wave of her hand. He saluted with his flashlight, squared his shoulders, and tramped off down the yard. He was immediately engulfed in a sheet of wind-driven rain.

The three girls crept along the wall of the house until they reached the corner. They huddled together there, hands in pockets, straining to catch a glimpse of Georgie's light.

"There's too much rain! We'll never see him!" cried Shelley.

"Can't you do something?" Carrie leaned around Shelley and touched the wand bulging under Lucy's jacket. "With that?"

"I'll try," agreed Lucy, and she drew the wand out and pressed the tiny golden flower. The wand snapped to full length and gleamed a rich black in the beam of Shelley's flashlight. A bold streak of lightning jagged across the sky and was mirrored along the length of the wand. Lucy flinched, but continued to raise her right arm steadily until the wand was pointed in the direction of the Jacobsen cellar.

Lucy began to move the tip of the wand in a small circle. The wind and the rain snatched at the wand, but she continued the circling movement and gradually the rain began to clear in that one spot: a small round window at one end of a calm, clear tunnel through the rain. At the other end of the tunnel they could see the flicker of light that was Georgie's flashlight, moving through the rough underbrush that hid the cellar. At last the light stopped in one spot and moved steadily from right to left and then up and down.

"My arm's getting tired." Lucy steadied her right arm with her left. Carrie moved to her side and helped support the arm too.

"The rain is leaking in. Hurry!" urged Lucy.

Shelley quickly moved off toward Georgie's distant light, counting the steps as she went. Carrie and Lucy paced off the steps behind her.

"Twenty-two, twenty-three, twenty-four," they chanted together.

On the last step, Lucy dropped the arm that held the wand and the little clear tunnel through the rain collapsed.

Carrie began to dig. The rain washed the dirt back into the hole almost as fast as she dug it out, but gradually the hole grew deeper. The wind added to their difficulty; it whirled and snatched at them, howling in their ears, driving the rain into their eyes and whipping the breath from their mouths. The three girls could barely see each other.

"I can't," gasped Carrie, resting from her digging. "There's nothing."

At their feet, lit by the dim yellow beam of Shelley's flashlight, the hole began to fill with muddy water.

"It's no use," Carrie shouted against the wind.

"What? What's the matter?" Georgie stumbled from the howling darkness that surrounded them.

Shelley pointed to the rapidly filling hole. "We've dug deep. There isn't anything there."

They all looked at Lucy.

Lucy drew the red knobby lump from her pocket and held it out in front of her chest. It took both hands to hold the heavy glass. It was glowing a soft red.

"Follow me," Lucy ordered, and began to walk in a large circle around the hole Carrie had dug. As she walked, the red glow from the remains of the fire creature became a wide flat ribbon that flowed out and away from Lucy and then doubled back and lay flat on the ground. Lucy stepped onto this ribbon and so did the others. Around they paced, laying down the ribbon of light, stepping out a glowing circle.

When they arrived back at the beginning, Lucy gave the lump a swift flick to the side and the luminous ribbon was broken. Then she pocketed the lump and stepped inside the glowing circle, motioning the others to do the same.

Quickly she drew out the wand and placed the extended tip of it on the circle where the beginning of the bright ribbon met its end. Slowly Lucy lifted the wand up, up and up, and as the tip rose it drew the light up with it—not just at that point but all around the circle. A wall of soft red light rose, pulled up by the tip of the wand.

Lucy's right arm trembled with the weight of the lifting, but she set her chin and raised the wand even further, up and up and over. At last the walls met as she lifted the wand directly over her head. The four children stood enclosed in a softly glowing dome of light that protected them from the storm.

"That's better," Lucy muttered, collapsing the wand. "Shelley, where do you think we should dig?"

"Me?" Shelley was astounded by the dome. She wanted to touch it but was afraid. Georgie wasn't. He tapped the structure with his finger.

"Papery! M-m-m-m-m."

"Yes." Lucy looked tired. Her face was pale and her eyes huge. "You must find the Orb and the Crown."

Shelley began to pace the sodden earth inside the dome. Now that the rain and wind were shut out, it was easy to see what lay at their feet.

"Here's the remains of a corner post." She pointed to a jagged stump. "The white stones are gone, though." She dropped to her knees and began to examine the earth carefully.

"Shelley! Hurry!" Lucy was very pale in the beam of Georgie's flashlight.

A sudden picture of the frozen whirling tornadoes filled Shelley's mind. She searched faster, harder.

"Please," she breathed and there, off to the side, something caught her eye. She pounced on it. It was a tiny white flower.

"Here!" she crowed. "Dig here!"

Carrie began to dig where Shelley pointed. Georgie and Lucy knelt beside the rapidly growing hole, scooping out the earth with their hands.

Shelley stood a moment, gazing at the flower that was quickly wilting, cupped in her hands. "Thank you, Rowan," she murmured. She carefully wrapped the flower in her handkerchief and put it deep in her inside pocket. Then she, too, knelt beside the hole and helped dig.

At last the spade thunked against wood and Georgie drew up the box. He opened it and unwrapped the Crown. Lucy put it on her head, then pulled her hood up over it and tied the string tightly under her chin.

She lifted the Orb before her in her two hands.

"Wow!" Georgie's excited whisper hissed around the dome. "Look at them go!"

The colored spirals within the Orb were spinning rapidly.

"It is almost time," Lucy said and stowed the glass ball in her pocket. Her jacket was dragged down with the weight of the Orb on one side and the heavy remains of the fire creature in the other. She gripped the wand in her right hand, eyes huge and serious in a white face.

"Now we must go," she announced. "Now we must go to the high place." She lifted the wand and the dome disappeared. The savage storm fell upon them.

Later, after it was all over, Shelley was to look back upon that journey and marvel that they were able to complete it.

"A terrible struggle," she wrote in the Rellard notebook.

They found that the torrents of rain had swollen the river beyond its banks and forced it through to the old channel that had prevailed before erosion from Hawker Rock had pushed the river into a great curve. That meant that the old road and the old bridge were under water.

"We'll have to go around the long way. The new bridge should be okay," Georgie shouted to them and they tramped along the higher road. But even the new bridge was threatened by the rising water, which was surging high on the supports.

"Hurry!" Lucy shouted. "The dam!"

Georgie was inclined to argue about the dam. "The dam's safe!" he insisted, but hurried along over the bridge behind the girls.

The road rose sharply in front of them and no one had breath for talking. Lucy pushed ahead, wand clenched in her hand.

Suddenly, above the noise of the storm there rose another sound, a horrible grinding rush. Lucy turned and pointed down the hill to the bridge below them.

"The dam," she said flatly.

The dreadful rush of noise rose, and out of the rain and wind a wall of muddy water appeared, sweeping down the swollen river. On it came, a boiling tumble of destruction, which engulfed the bridge and surged on.

Georgie was stunned. "It just . . ."—he held out a hand, searching for a word—". . . just crumpled!" He dropped his hand.

Spreading above the Rock before them, a deep

copper hue began to permeate the sky. A new note was added to the torrent of noise created by the storm, a rising strident note.

"They are moving," Lucy announced. "They are marching again!"

The four children resumed their climb to the top of Hawker Rock. In the end, it was Carrie who bore the full weight of Lucy up the last difficult scramble.

Finally they stood, buffeted by the wind and rain, threatened by the lightning, and surveyed the scene that they had previously seen in miniature, whirling within the glowing remains of the fire creature.

For once Georgie was speechless.

The sky to the northwest was heaped with heavy black clouds. Moving toward the children, and the town, which lay behind them, were the tornadoes. Three stood in front and one, larger and blacker, towered behind. Where the funnels touched the ground, there were explosions of earth, trees and buildings. The four dark whirling towers of destruction were accompanied by a grating roar, a fearful sound—beyond wind and rain, beyond gales—a blast of elemental fury.

Lucy undid her hood and let it fall to her shoulders. The Crown gleamed dully on her forehead. She pulled the red knobby lump from her pocket and placed it on the ground before her.

"You stand here, Carrie." She pointed to a spot about two paces from the red lump. "You are the back-up person." Carrie stood.

In front of Carrie she arranged Georgie and Shelley, side by side. "Hold hands," she directed and the brother and sister stood hand in hand.

"Now," Lucy said, and placed herself in front of Georgie and Shelley. "If I fall, catch me in your arms!" she called over her shoulder. "And whatever happens, don't lose the Orb!"

"Okay!" Georgie yelled.

The noise from the approaching tornadoes was deafening, and the change in air pressure was causing their ears to pop. A frantic high note was added to the tornadoes' dreadful song.

Lucy turned to face the whirling funnels. At her feet, the remains of the fire beast glowed. In her left hand, held high, the spirals of color swirled in the Orb, emitting a splendid energy. Her right hand, the withered crippled hand, gripped the fully extended wand. Lucy pointed it at the oncoming funnels.

"I am the Rellard, Keeper of the Power!" she shouted into the roar. "In the name of the Power of the Water, I command you to stop!"

The sheets of rain that had lashed and whipped around the children began to abate. Shelley blinked the rain from her eyes and Georgie licked his lips.

"Come on, stop, you!" whispered Carrie, but the furious advance of the tornadoes continued.

Lucy raised her voice again. "I command you, in the name of the Power of the Fire!"

The glassy red lump began to grow and send out tendrils of flame. Shelley gasped as the fire beast rose before them, standing on its hind legs and roaring its fury at the whirling funnels.

But they did not stop. They were getting very close now, ripping up the highway that led to the town. A red pick-up truck was caught in the tip of one funnel and disappeared.

Lucy raised the Orb and wand higher.

"With the Power of the Leaf and the Rock, I command you!"

Georgie noticed a deeper note in Lucy's voice. He gripped Shelley's hand tighter, and braced himself.

The children felt the rock and earth shift beneath their feet as a section of Hawker Rock slid down into the river. The earth, rocks, and fallen trees created a dam that stemmed the rush of flood water, spreading it harmlessly into the fields beyond the town.

But the four funnels drew inexorably closer. Their combined roar was now almost deafening as they raged through the outskirts of the town, tearing into a barn, flattening a shed, tossing a gasoline pump into the air.

Still higher Lucy raised the Orb, whose spirals were now a whirling blur of color. The wand gleamed in the flickering lightning.

"I command you, with the Power of the Claw and Feather," intoned Lucy. The funnels were almost upon them now. She raised her arms almost straight up, a defiant figure silhouetted against the towering funnels. A tawny owl flew raggedly through the buffeting wind and perched on Lucy's head.

"Owl!" exclaimed Georgie. "My owl!"

The owl swiveled its head and winked a greeting.

The four children could hardly stand now against the force of the wind. Carrie supported Shelley and Georgie with her hands on their shoulders. They, in turn, braced themselves as Lucy was forced back against their linked arms. The fire beast was spread low and the owl's feathers fluttered and flattened.

Lucy shouted, her voice deep and resonant. "I command you as Rellard, Keeper of the Power! I command you to go back whence you came! Go!" and Lucy flung her arms forward, throwing the Power of the wand and the Orb at the four advancing funnels.

A furious shriek arose from the tornadoes, but Lucy held firm.

"Go! Go!" she chanted, thrusting the Power in the face of the whirling darkness.

"Go! Go!" Shelley and Georgie chanted. Carrie squeezed her eyes shut and opened her mouth wide. "Go!" she yelled.

The whirlwinds stopped their forward movement and stood shrieking their defiance. They were crowned with jagged bolts of lightning. Their fury was terrible.

"I command you, for the last time. In the name of the Power of the Rellard, go!"

A tremendous blaze of lightning forked from the black towers of wind and leaped to the wand in Lucy's hand. For a small space in time, Lucy quivered on the end of the jag of lightning; then, without a sound, she fell into the arms of her brother and sister. The tips of the whirlwinds lifted from the earth and retreated slowly up into the clouds. The furious roar fell away and peace descended. Carrie, Georgie, and Shelley gazed down at the limp and twisted figure of Lucy.

The Crown had fallen from her head and the Orb was shattered into small pieces, its luminous whirling stopped forever. The wand was a tortured scrap of metal, still clutched in Lucy's right hand.

Without a word, Carrie knelt and gathered Lucy in her arms. Georgie and Shelley helped her stand.

"Come on," said Carrie. "Let's go home."

Things were in a terrible mess for a while.

Lucy was whisked away to the hospital and Mum and Dad rushed home from the city to be at her bedside.

"She's in a coma, with one *m*," Georgie explained to everyone. "Two *m*'s make a comma. That's a kind of punctuation." Shelley knew that Georgie was very worried about Lucy, that's why he talked that way. She stayed close to him.

Carrie was looking after them at her place. On the second afternoon after the storm, they sat huddled together around the table in the Carney kitchen, waiting for word about Lucy. Georgie made it to the phone before it could ring a second time.

"It's Mum!" he yelled, and hunched eagerly over the telephone, coaxing the message from the receiver with nods, smiles, and a final "Bye! Yes, yes! Tell her we miss her!" He stood and faced the two girls, his face straining under his grin. "She's going to be okay. Lucy's going to be fine! Mum said." His grin became wry. "She said that Lucy has turned the corner!"

"We'd better go clean up that mess the fire made," said Carrie.

Everyone else was cleaning up the mess left by the terrible storm. Debris was everywhere—trees torn from the earth, telephone poles felled, wrack left behind by the receding waters of the flooded river— the whole town was shoveling, scrubbing, hacking away at the mess.

That evening Shelley and Georgie, along with all the Carneys, watched an interview with a meteorologist on television who answered questions about the appalling force of the tornadoes, all except for the last question.

"I really can't answer that," he said, blinking against the glare of the sunshine. He had been interviewed while standing on top of Hawker Rock. "I can't tell you why those tornadoes stopped moving toward the town. They just stopped. Right about here, as a matter of fact," and he pointed toward the place where the funnels had lifted into the clouds.

"The storm must have released vast quantities of energy and burned itself out," he continued. "Look at this charred area over here."

The television camera dutifully panned over the rocks and grass and focused on the blackened, blasted spot where Lucy had stood.

Georgie and Shelley and Carrie looked at one another with studiously blank faces. Without a word, they rose and waded out of the huddle of Carney boys and trailed out through the kitchen and across the lawns toward the house next door.

"Hey! Somebody's home!" shouted Georgie, spotting the car in the driveway. He ran ahead.

"Everybody's home!" he yelled, running back to the two girls. "Even Lucy!"

And she was. A pale, wan Lucy propped up in her bed, smiling at them from the pillows.

"Can I have owl in here?" she asked. Georgie galloped off, bumping wildly out of the room, yelling, "Sure. You can have old owl!" at the top of his voice.

Carrie smiled. "Hey, Lucy, it's great to see you!" and then turned to go. "See you," she flipped over her shoulder, and collided with Georgie and the owl as they rushed back through the door.

Lucy held out both arms.

"Thank you." She smiled.

Carrie, Georgie and Shelley stood staring at Lucy —at her arms, at her right arm.

"What's the matter?" asked Lucy.

"Your arm. It's . . . it's . . ." Georgie was stumped.

"It got burned a little bit, here." Lucy showed the palm of her hand. "That's why the bandages."

"Yes, but . . ." Shelley sat down on the bed beside Lucy. "It's straighter, and . . . and . . . fatter!"

Lucy grinned. *"And* it works better. See?" She flexed her fingers gently. "All that electricity did something to it. Doctor MacCreath said it was something about nervous . . ."

"Nerves," interrupted Georgie.

" . . . and regen something, I forget . . ."

"Probably regeneration. That means . . ."

It was Lucy's turn to interrupt Georgie. "Anyway, Doctor MacCreath said that I need to exercise it and that it probably will be as good as new!" She smiled, and then grew serious. "Almost, anyway. I'll have scars, he said. Especially here," and she pointed to the palm of her right hand.

"Now, give me owl," commanded Lucy, and Georgie handed her the bird.

Days later Georgie came to Shelley, frowning his consternation.

"Shelley, just look at this, will you?"

"It's the Rellard comic, isn't it? It looks like Scorpion Man to me, but it's the Rellard one, isn't it?"

"Well, I thought it was. It was where I always hid the Rellard comic." Georgie frowned even harder and bit his lip.

"But now it isn't, is that it?" asked Shelley.

Georgie nodded. "It's about some genius scientist that invents all sorts of things." Georgie pushed his glasses firmly up on his nose. "He's named Creaton."

"It must be all over now," said Shelley.

"Yep. All over," and Georgie walked away, reading the comic.

"I'd better get all this written down," thought Shelley and went to find the Rellard notebook. She wrote for a long time and when she reached the last page, she closed the notebook and sat considering the sketch of the Rellard man on the front. Then she walked to the sunroom window and looked out.

Lucy was playing happily in the sandpunt. The trunk of the Big Tree had thrown up many new green shoots, which gleamed in the sunlight. Lucy's arms were brown and strong as she molded another sand ball. Georgie was pumping up a pail of water. Another war with the Carney boys was pending.

"Anyway, our part of it is over," and, placing the notebook on the windowsill beside a pot in which a tall lily bloomed, Shelley ran out to join her brother and sister.